HARLEQUIN®
Presents~

Outside, the weather is getting hotter, and here at
Harlequin Presents, we've got the books to warm
the temperature inside, too!

Don't miss the final story in Sharon Kendrick's
fabulous THE DESERT PRINCES trilogy—
The Desert King's Virgin Bride—where Sheikh Malik
seduces an innocent Englishwoman. And what
happens when a divorced couple discover their
desire for each other hasn't faded? Read
The Pregnancy Affair by Anne Mather to find out!

Our gorgeous billionaires will get your hearts racing....
Emma Darcy brings you a sizzling slice of Sydney life
with *The Billionaire's Scandalous Marriage*, when
Damien Wynter is determined that Charlotte be
his bride—*and* the mother of his child! In
Lindsay Armstrong's *The Australian's Housekeeper
Bride*, a wealthy businessman needs a wife—and he
chooses his housekeeper! In Carole Mortimer's
Wife by Contract, Mistress by Demand, brooding
billionaire Rufus uses a marriage of convenience to
bed Gabriella.

For all of you who love our Greek tycoons, you won't
be disappointed this ~~~~~~~~~~~~~~~~~~~~~~~~~ *ient
Wife* by Jacqueline ~~~~~~~~~~~~~~~~~~~~~~~~~~
Helen an experience~~~~~~~~~~~~~~~~~~~~~~~~~ g
night. Chantelle Sha~~~~~~~~~~~~~~~~~~~~~~~~ ls
the story of a P.A. w~~~~~~~~~~~~~~~~~~~~~~~
love with her hands~~~~~~~~~~~~~~~~~~~~~~~~
love some Italian passion, Susan Stephens's *In the
Venetian's Bed* brings you Luca Barbaro, a sexy and
ruthless Venetian, whom Nell just can't resist.

*Legally wed,
but he's never said,
"I love you."
They're...*

*The series where marriages are made
in haste...and love comes later....*

*Look out for more WEDLOCKED!
wedding stories available only from
Harlequin Presents®.*

Lindsay Armstrong

THE AUSTRALIAN'S HOUSEKEEPER BRIDE

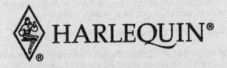

TORONTO • NEW YORK • LONDON
AMSTERDAM • PARIS • SYDNEY • HAMBURG
STOCKHOLM • ATHENS • TOKYO • MILAN • MADRID
PRAGUE • WARSAW • BUDAPEST • AUCKLAND

ISBN-13: 978-0-373-12634-7
ISBN-10: 0-373-12634-4

THE AUSTRALIAN'S HOUSEKEEPER BRIDE

First North American Publication 2007.

Copyright © 2007 by Lindsay Armstrong.

www.eHarlequin.com

Printed in U.S.A.

All about the author...
Lindsay Armstrong

I was born in South Africa, but I'm now an Australian citizen, with a New Zealand–born husband. We had an epic introduction to Australia. We landed in Perth then drove around the "top end" with four kids under the age of eight. There were some marvelous times and wonderful sights, and we've been fascinated by wild Australia ever since. We've done quite a bit of exploring the coastline by boat, including one amazing trip to The Kimberley.

We've also farmed and trained racehorses. After our fifth child was born, I started to write. It was something I'd always wanted to do, but never seemed to know how to start. Then one day I sat down at the kitchen table with an abandoned exercise book, suddenly convinced the time had come to stop dreaming about it and start doing it. That book never got published, but it certainly opened the floodgates!

PROLOGUE

RHIANNON FAIRFAX shared a taxi one day with a man to die for. She was twenty-two at the time.

It was during a massive Sydney thunderstorm and it was to prove a memorable ride.

They met on a rain-drenched pavement in the city. He had an umbrella, she was smothered in a bright yellow hooded plastic raincoat. He'd been there first, but when she and a taxi arrived almost simultaneously she wiped the rain out of her eyes and asked him above the din of the downpour if they could share it. Because her other options appeared to include being washed away and she was also running late.

He agreed and they went through the awkward business of getting his umbrella down and getting themselves into the taxi while the driver grumbled about them flooding the back seat.

'Phew!' Rhiannon pushed her hood back, uncovering a navy beret pulled down over her ears with all her hair tucked up into it. She didn't normally wear it like that but she was cold and that was the only way she could keep it on under the hood. 'What a day!'

Her companion regarded her quizzically. 'At least you're dressed for it.'

She fingered the beret and grimaced. 'Warmth and dryness take precedence over looks at the moment. So where are you headed?'

He told her and they consulted the driver and worked out that he would be dropped off first.

Then she sat back as the taxi, its windscreen wipers working overtime, pulled out into the slick grey canyon of the street and she looked at her companion properly for the first time.

Rhiannon's eyebrows rose slowly, almost until they were touching the beret, as she took him in. Tall, dark and handsome multiplied by a factor of ten summed it up, she decided. Thick dark hair, deep blue eyes, slightly hollow cheeks and aquiline features that gave him an aloof air, broad shoulders beneath the jacket of a superbly tailored though now damp charcoal suit...

He looked to be in his early thirties. He looked— she tried to sum it up—the embodiment of someone who wielded power in a boardroom. Yet there was a tantalising aura of a man who would be good at other things.

What things, she wondered? And how had she got that impression? From his physique, his long, strong hands, his tan?

Then she realised he was returning her gaze enigmatically.

'Sorry,' she murmured with a rueful little smile, 'but you must be used to it.'

His lips twisted. 'I could probably say the same for you, except there's not a lot to see.' His gaze drifted down the voluminous raincoat that fell almost to her feet.

She wasn't sure why she felt so chatty with a perfect stranger, except for the fact that her life had taken an upward turn only about half an hour ago. 'I suppose you're very much spoken for?'

He settled those impressive shoulders against the seat. 'I'm not, as it happens. I'm actually sworn off being "spoken for" at the moment and possibly the duration.'

'Oh, dear, what a shame.' Rhiannon eyed him concernedly. 'If you're serious?'

For a fleeting moment his mouth hardened then he shrugged and turned the question. 'How about you?'

'Actually,' Rhiannon looked away and pleated the yellow plastic of her raincoat, unaware of the air of vulnerability that overcame her, 'I'm pretty sure I'm sworn off men for life.'

He watched her busy fingers. 'How come?'

'You wouldn't want to know.' She made a determined effort not to go down that road again. 'So what were we talking about before?'

He looked into her sparkling brown eyes. 'I was trying to pay you a compliment in return for the one you paid me.'

'Well, I don't think I'm a ten,' she replied, 'but I do have some good points. My figure's not bad, I'm actually a natural blonde under this thing,' she pointed to her beret, 'if you go for them—but if there's one thing I'm sinfully proud of maybe, it's my legs.'

He raised an eyebrow. 'Why sinfully?'

'Legs is as legs does,' she recited and rubbed the bridge of her nose. 'It's your soul that counts.'

'Let me guess, the preaching of your convent school?' he hazarded.

Rhiannon laughed. 'In my last year at my convent school, my Mother Superior was convinced my legs were going to lead me on a downward path. On the other hand, my next school took a different view. They were of the opinion they were a great asset.'

'Next school?' He frowned.

'I had a rather extended education,' she said quickly.

'If I could see your legs, I might be able to—settle the dispute. That is,' his deep blue eyes were grave but not so grave as to hide the wicked little glint in them, 'advise you whether it's sinful to be proud of them or not.'

'Well,' she said, 'if nothing else I think we should take the driver's sensibilities into account, don't you?'

They'd left the city and were driving down a dripping, classy, tree-lined street in Woollahra, her companion's destination. When the driver didn't respond, it was only because, as they realised moments later, he'd lost control of the taxi as it planed through a sea of water.

They mounted the pavement and hit a tree. They bounced off the tree and crunched through a fence behind it and came to rest precariously at the top of a rocky incline that led down to a park.

The next few minutes were chaotic. The passengers discovered themselves to be uninjured but the driver was knocked out. How long they would balance at the angle at which they were tilted was a moot point.

So they scrambled out into the rain, used a mobile phone to call for help and began to get the driver out before the car rolled down the incline.

It was no easy task. The impact had buckled the driver's door and, had Rhiannon's companion not been very strong but also extremely quick-thinking and resourceful, they'd have lost the driver and his taxi down the rocks.

They laid him on the grass, still out cold, on a waterproof sheet they'd found in the boot and Rhiannon ripped off her raincoat and covered him with it.

They were both, by this time, muddy, scratched, dirty and soaked.

The taxi settled then quite slowly slid down the rocks to bury its nose in the park.

'Thank heavens we got him out!' she breathed. 'Are you all right? You've cut your hand and you've ruined your jacket.'

'I'm OK. I— Ah!' They both turned at the sound of sirens and in short order a police car and an ambulance arrived. Before long they'd been reassured that the taxi driver was not seriously injured.

By the time they'd both given their details to the police, Rhiannon to a policewoman who'd taken pity on her and invited her into the police car, Rhiannon was aware she was running very late so she explained her situation to the policewoman and asked her to call another taxi.

It came almost immediately, a miracle on a day like that, probably something to do with being summoned by the police.

She climbed out of the police car and the man she'd shared the first taxi with turned to her, having given his details to the second police officer.

'Would you like to share it?' she asked. 'Unfortunately I'm running terribly late now, so—but...' She hesitated with real anxiety written large in her eyes.

'Thank you, no. I'm nearly there so I'll walk.'

'Well, let me pay my share of the first ride, not that I have any idea what it is, but—' She flicked her purse open.

He closed his uncut hand over hers. 'It's on me and I won't take no for an answer.'

She looked down at the lean, tanned hand over hers and felt an unmistakable *frisson* run through her.

She tore her gaze away and looked up into his eyes.

'As for your legs,' he said, and flicked a dark blue look down her short tight skirt to her feet, 'you're right, they're sensational.'

'I didn't say that,' she protested, going pink.

'No, of course not, you simply drew my attention to them.' He shrugged. 'I'm not complaining about that at all.'

She blushed more vividly and he smiled at her, suddenly and unexpectedly, such a breathtakingly, purely wicked masculine smile it put her into a worse fluster.

'Well, good-goodbye, then,' she stammered. 'I do have to dash.'

He waited as she stood rooted to the spot for a moment before shaking herself and scrambling into the second taxi.

When she got home she rushed in but her father was exactly where she'd left him, watching television.

She heaved a sigh of relief, kissed the top of his head and went away to shower and change.

The sight that greeted her in her bedroom mirror caused her to close her eyes in frustration. She'd forgotten about the wretched beret she was wearing pulled down to her ears and for a moment she almost didn't recognise herself. It certainly was about as unflattering a frame for her face as she could think of.

She ripped it off and her silky fair hair made a much better frame. Still, how mortifying to meet a man to die for looking like that?

Then the irony of it all claimed her. If anyone had reason to be turned off men, she did. So what had happened to her in the taxi?

CHAPTER ONE

FOUR years later it was an older and wiser Rhiannon Fairfax who found herself staring wide-eyed at a man in an airport lounge.

Her flight was delayed and she was feeling bored and restless.

He *was*, she supposed, a striking example of the male species. He was tall and dark and she got a glimpse of aquiline features. His physique was superb, wide-shouldered and sleek-hipped beneath designer jeans, a white shirt and a leather jacket that shouted expense and quality craftsmanship.

He was the man she'd shared a taxi with four years ago, she was sure!

He had someone with him, almost as eye-catching as he was; a woman, tall, slim, dark and expensive-looking. She spoilt it with a slightly submissive air as she received what was obviously a string of instructions from him.

Then his briefing came to an end and he turned more towards Rhiannon and smiled, suddenly and unexpectedly, at the woman he was with. She blushed and looked for an instant as if she'd been transported to heaven, before taking her departure.

If there'd been any doubt in Rhiannon's mind, that smile banished it

But that was when he lifted his head and surveyed the crowded lounge with the smile gone.

She caught her breath at how well she remembered his dark blue eyes and that aloof air—although today it was more than that. He had the air of a man who took what he wanted when he wanted it and damn the consequences...

All the same, she felt herself smiling at the memory of that rain-soaked taxi trip.

Then she realised he was looking at *her*, and for a long moment she was flustered into immobility with the smile still etched on her lips.

He took his time as he examined her short though stylish fair hair, her figure beneath her grey, severely tailored trouser suit worn with a black blouse. It was such a long, slow assessment and so intimate, she broke out in goose-pimples.

Then he looked back into her eyes and, with a shrug, turned away.

Rhiannon felt herself blush vividly.

He obviously hadn't recognised her—perhaps it wasn't so surprising without that dreadful beret. But did she look like the kind of girl who made tacit passes at men?

She bit her lip suddenly. She'd certainly pursued an unusual line of conversation with a strange man in a taxi...

She was still smarting when the flight was called and she boarded economy class while her perfectly arrogant stranger disappeared into business class.

She tried to comfort herself with the thought that he probably had some short-comings like an unmasculine sort of vanity—it didn't altogether work but, by the time the flight landed on the Gold Coast, most of her equilibrium had been restored.

She'd spent the last half-hour concentrating on her new position. Put plainly, she was a housekeeper. Put more accurately, she specialised in putting her skills to work for the rich, and sometimes the famous, for short stints while she reorganized their households to maximum efficiency and style; or in some cases for a special event.

This wasn't what she'd set out to do with her life. For most of her childhood she'd been rich and her parents had been famous. Then it had all fallen apart, she'd lost her mother and been forced to make a living.

It had occurred to her that her time at an expensive finishing-school in Switzerland could be put to better use than its original purpose of "finishing" her to take her place in society.

The result was that now, at twenty-six, she had her own one-woman agency that specialised in passing her expertise in house management, style, cuisine— she was a passionate cook—on to others.

She rarely accepted assignments that were longer than a month. This one would be for that duration and she would be extremely well paid for it. She'd learnt not to sell herself cheap.

The assignment, the one she was flying to the Gold Coast for, was an interesting one.

Southall, the present family seat of the Richardsons, was a vast country mansion perched on the scenic rim of the Gold Coast. The Richardson family owned large tracts of Queensland grazing country as well as cattle stations in West Australia and the Northern Territory.

It was an old family and an extremely wealthy one.

And as its grazing empire had expanded, Southall, rural but with the advantage of being close to the coast, had been chosen as the family headquarters.

That had been in Ross and Margaret Richardson's time.

Then Margaret had died five years ago and Ross had remarried fairly swiftly, a woman young enough to be his daughter—Rhiannon knew this from the gossip columns. Ross had taken his second wife, Andrea Comero, a model, to the south of France to live. He'd handed over the reins to his elder son, Lee, who was unmarried. Ross had died less than a year ago.

Both his sons had been unmarried at the time of Ross's second marriage but the younger son, Matthew, had since made the trip to the altar with a gorgeous television starlet, Mary Wiseman. After a six-month honeymoon touring the world he had brought his bride to Southall.

Again, Rhiannon had gleaned this from the gossip columns but, while Margaret and Ross Richardson had been household names and faces, while Matt Richardson's marriage had achieved quite a bit of publicity, while Andrea Comero had been a well-known face, Rhiannon knew nothing at all about the elder son, Lee.

It was on Lee's behalf, however, that Rhiannon's services had been sought by his PA. With great diplomacy she'd been given to understand that Mary Richardson née Wiseman, in her early twenties, was not *au fait* with running a large household. She was, however, said to wish to return to Southall its reputation for providing great food, wonderfully comfortable beds and always interesting company that it had held in Margaret Richardson's day.

Where Lee Richardson himself came into it all, Rhiannon had no idea. Still, it was none of her business if he wanted his younger brother's wife to take over Southall. It was Rhiannon's windfall, in fact.

Rhiannon collected her luggage from the airport carousel then presented herself at the information desk, as she'd been instructed to do.

She was just about to give her name to one of the clerks, when a deep, husky voice beside her asked another clerk whether a Rhiannon Fairfax had made herself known to them.

She shut her mouth and turned to the speaker, only to stop as if shot. It was none other than the man from the taxi, the man who'd obviously mistaken the way she'd been looking and smiling at him in the airport lounge before the flight.

Her abrupt movement caught his eye, and he turned to her. Their gazes clashed.

'Well, well,' he drawled, 'if it isn't the lady who was trying to come on to me in Sydney, although "lady" may not be perfectly apt.' His gaze swept downwards.

Rhiannon opened her mouth a couple of times but nothing came out. Then she took hold and said icily, 'I was not trying to "come on to you", I would scorn,' her eyes flashed, 'to do that.'

'Could have fooled me, ma'am.' But he frowned suddenly.

'The thing is,' she persisted through her teeth, 'I happen to be Rhiannon Fairfax.'

Those rather amazing dark blue eyes narrowed. 'Now, that,' he said softly, 'should be really interesting, Ms Fairfax.'

'On the contrary—'

He overrode her smoothly. 'Because I happen to be
Lee Richardson, your—' he let the word hang in the
air '—employer.'

'Oh.' It was a singularly ineffective response,
Rhiannon was uncomfortably aware, but it was all she
was capable of at the time.

'Mmm…' he agreed with a lightening look of
wicked amusement. 'Perhaps you should bear in mind
that life can be littered with coincidences before you
eyes—'

'Don't go on,' she interrupted, 'unless you'd like me
to turn around and go straight back to Sydney?'

'I'm afraid you can't, ma'am,' said one of the wildly
interested clerks who'd been following the exchange
word for word. 'The last flight left half an hour ago.'

'I can spend the night in a motel, then—'

'You can't,' Lee Richardson said, 'because—'

'Will you both stop telling me what I can't do?' She
eyed him and the clerk with exasperation.

'What I meant was,' Lee Richardson amended
gravely, 'that I'm your lift up to Southall—when the
flight was delayed and it was realised we were both on
it, I was deputised to drive you up.'

'What's that got to do with anything?' Rhiannon
raised an eyebrow at him.

'Nothing. But we desperately need you up there,
Ms Fairfax. My sister-in-law is throwing a party the
night after tomorrow that could, by all accounts, be a
disaster.'

Rhiannon blinked. 'How so?'

'She gave the caterers the wrong day. They're
booked up for the right day, a Sunday, anyway. So, it
would appear, is every other decent caterer on the
coast. Of course, it may be beyond you to organise

drinks and a buffet supper for thirty people at such short notice.' He looked at her expressionlessly.

'Providing I had access to shops, I could do it in my sleep,' Rhiannon said gently.

Lee Richardson summed her up from head to toe. She was medium height, five feet five-to-six probably, and her figure was deliciously curvy beneath the grey suit and black blouse. Her straight, smooth fair hair was expertly cut to chin length and parted on one side. The longer side arched attractively against her face. She had rather unusual light brown eyes emphasised by long, carefully darkened lashes.

The rest of her make-up was light and flawless, so was her skin, her lips were luscious and gleamed a frosted coral-pink.

Was it his imagination, though, or had he met her before? Something in her voice and those sparkling brown eyes seemed to strike a chord but he couldn't place it.

More to the point, could she ever look entirely businesslike? he reflected. Would that glossy, rather gorgeous air, those curves, always get in the way of taking her seriously?

She wasn't what he'd expected. She definitely wasn't the dragon-like person he'd visualised, who could impose their personality on a household that bore all the hallmarks of descending into a dysfunctional mess.

Although, Lee conceded, she had been quite cool under fire, so to speak; she might even be more interesting than his first impressions of her had indicated. But that brought up another query. She *had* been staring and smiling at him in a way that experience had shown him women did when they were analysing his potential in bed and out of it.

On the other hand, her wounded vanity might work to his advantage and things were in crisis.

Following this line of thought, he said drily at last, 'I wonder.'

'Then I'll prove it to you, Mr Richardson,' Rhiannon replied with a strange little glint in her sherry-brown eyes.

A muscle moved in his cheek, as if he was trying not to smile.

'But don't congratulate yourself on the fact that I walked into a trap of your making,' she advised with obvious satire.

He raised an eyebrow at her. 'No?'

'No,' Rhiannon agreed. 'Look at it like this: I feel for your sister-in-law so I'll help out with the party. I'm just as liable to pack my bags and go home the next day, however.'

'Yes, sir,' Lee Richardson said. 'Please don't take that the wrong way, Ms Fairfax,' he added. 'It's only meant to imply that I've changed my mind—you could be exactly what we need at Southall. Let's go.'

Rhiannon was still simmering as the powerful four-wheel-drive vehicle Lee Richardson drove climbed the range from the coast to the hinterland.

Indeed, part of her was deeply regretting the fact that she hadn't flung his job back in his face but it wasn't a mystery to her why she hadn't. She needed the money, she rather desperately these days needed every dollar she could earn...

It was dark so she couldn't take in the countryside as she thought her painful thoughts, although it was obvious the road was steep and winding.

Unfortunately, the dark also seemed to encapsulate

her and Lee Richardson in a bubble where it was impossible for her not to be conscious of him in a rather disturbing way...

His hands were lean and powerful on the wheel—what kind of havoc would they wreak on her naked body? she found herself wondering again, to her dismay.

His profile was clean-cut, his shoulders, beneath the expensive leather, were tantalisingly broad and straight and he changed gear and drove the car with the flair and authority that somehow suggested to her he would demonstrate the same flair and authority in bed...

She closed her eyes and went hot and cold as this occurred to her.

Fortunately, not much later, they turned off the main road, drove down several tree-lined side-roads and came to impressive wrought-iron gates set in a high stone wall.

They opened silently at the press of a button in the car.

'We're here, Miss Fairfax,' he murmured as he drove into a four-car garage. 'You're very quiet,' he added as he opened his door and the overhead light came on.

'I'm wondering what I've got myself into, to be honest,' she replied.

He half smiled. 'The nature of what you do—rescuing households from chaos—must often provide surprises.'

She regarded him steadily. 'Yes, but if you must know my...' She broke off. She'd been about to say 'my *latest* impressions' but she amended it to, 'My impressions of you, Mr Richardson, are not exactly favourable.'

'Listen, Rhiannon, you were the one who was staring and smiling at me in an unmistakable way,' he retorted. 'Any *impressions* you have of me flowed on directly from that.'

'All right, I was staring and smiling at you but it wasn't what you thought. It was because we've met before.'

He frowned and concentrated on her face then his eyes widened and he looked down at her trouser-clad legs. 'What a pity,' he said slowly, as his eyes came back to hers, 'you aren't wearing a skirt. I feel sure I would have recognised you immediately.'

She could tell that he was looking back down four years. Rhiannon flinched inwardly as she remembered with great clarity how she'd been rooted to the spot after he'd smiled at her.

'I object to being summed up as a pair of legs,' she said, anything to deflect *his* memories of the moment plus some genuine indignation.

'You brought up the subject of your legs in that taxi.'

She shrugged. 'I'm a different me now.'

'That's rather obvious,' he commented. 'No longer a chatty, bubbly girl perhaps.'

'I am four years older.'

'Is it that long ago?'

She nodded. 'But to be perfectly honest I know why I was feeling bubbly that day—I'd just got rather a good job.'

She grimaced. 'But I still can't work out—' she gestured with some humour '—how I got on to that tack.'

'An instantaneous attraction?' he suggested. 'Despite claiming to be turned off all men.'

She studied him for a moment. His thick dark hair was straight and lay on his forehead. A little network of lines creased attractively beside his eyes when he laughed. His skin was tanned and, although he was clean-shaven, he'd probably look sensational with designer stubble; look dangerous, moody, gloriously sexy and desirable…

'Uh—' she reined in her thoughts with an inward frown '—no—yes. I mean to say I'm still turned off men, Mr Richardson. How about you? I gather you're still "unspoken for"?'

'You gather right,' he said easily. 'So what was it, then?'

She studied her hands then shrugged. 'Just one of those things. Look,' she swept her hair back from her face with her forefinger, not to know at all that it was the first time Lee Richardson not only saw the gesture but also found it got to him in a way he was hard put to describe, 'may I make a request?'

His eyes narrowed and he hesitated briefly, then, 'Go ahead.'

'Can we put it all behind us? It *was* just one of those things and, if you really want me to get stuck in and sort out your home life, the best way is for us to make a fresh start.'

He considered several things. That she had a way of tilting her chin that gave her an almost regal air. That her straight little nose would have been haughty had it not been accompanied by a mouth that was anything but.

On the other hand, in light of what she'd been hired to do, a complicated-enough situation in its own right, he'd be mad to invite further complications.

'All right,' he said coolly and shrugged as he got out of the car.

Rhiannon took an unexpected breath because, as he closed his door, it was a bit like having a private door closed in her face. Why should it make her feel so curiously rebuffed?

There was a surprise waiting for them.

The house was in darkness and locked.

Lee Richardson frowned then retrieved his keys from his pocket and unlocked the heavy wooden front door. He led Rhiannon through the marble-tiled hall, switching on lights as they went, and into the kitchen.

It was a large, modern kitchen with black mottled granite counters and a commercial-size range and refrigeration—Rhiannon noted these things instinctively. There was a box pine table surrounded by six ladder-back chairs and there were some colourful pot plants.

Lee Richardson put his keys down beside a phone on one of the counters, and pressed the message button that was blinking frenziedly.

It was a long message that came through and the caller, a man, sounded agitated.

'Lee, Matt here, Mary's done a bit of a bunk. I think she was really gutted about getting the caterers mixed up and she's gone home to her mother. All she'll say is she's quite sure you and the super-housekeeper or whatever she is will be able to organise things much better than she could so she'll leave it all up to you both. I don't fly in from Perth until Sunday afternoon but I'll pick her up from her Mum's then and bring her up…'

There was a pause then Matt Richardson continued, 'Don't be too hard on her, bro, she is pregnant and maybe that's panicking her too. And I know you can handle the blasted party, somehow. Bye. Oh, by the way, the numbers may have grown.' Click.

Lee Richardson swore softly.

'Oh, dear,' Rhiannon said. 'Perhaps she's left a guest list?'

'Entirely too sane and sensible for Mary to think of that,' he said grimly then shrugged. 'So. Would you like a drink?'

Rhiannon pulled out a chair and sank into it. 'A glass of wine wouldn't go amiss if you've got one.'

'I have a whole cellarful but there should be some chilled in the fridge.'

There was and he poured a glass for her. He mixed himself a Scotch and water.

He said, as he sat down opposite her, 'Has this ever happened to you before, Ms Fairfax?'

She wrinkled her nose. 'No. But it's not insurmountable. Pregnancy *can* produce some curious mood swings,' she murmured almost to herself—then added swiftly, 'I believe she's also an actress?'

He stared at her rather penetratingly before saying, 'Yes.' He sat back and shoved his hands into his pockets. 'What I'd really like to do is call the whole thing off.'

'Do you think that's a good idea? Mightn't it reinforce your obvious disapproval of your sister-in-law?'

A rapier-like blue gaze came her way then Lee Richardson smiled reluctantly. 'Is it that apparent?'

'I'm afraid so.'

'I see why you're good at this kind of thing. Cool and logical. Funnily enough,' he looked amused, 'I wouldn't have taken you for such a cool, logical girl four years ago.'

Rhiannon moved a little uncomfortably.

'On the other hand I did find you charming,' he said. 'And forthright.'

'I don't suppose you're ever going to let me live that down,' she said tartly then looked more uncomfortable. 'Not that any "ever" is going to be involved.' She took a sip of wine and added, 'Just the duration of the job.'

He squared his shoulders and studied her comprehensively until she broke out into goose-pimples at the way that dark blue gaze slid over her upper body. Then he drawled, 'Do you really think so?'

Rhiannon's nose took on a slightly pinched look. 'I know so!' She drained her glass and said coolly, 'Are you doing the party or not?'

He considered. 'Yes.'

'Then would you mind if I had a look around, just to assess the facilities?'

'Be my guest, but I'll show you to your bedroom first.'

Rhiannon woke the next morning at five o'clock, as the sun was just climbing over the horizon, and took a few minutes to collect her thoughts.

Southall itself was beautiful, even from the impressions she'd got in the dark last night.

The house had sandstone walls beneath a vast shingle roof. Fluted columns supported the veranda roof, some of them smothered with flowering creepers—heavenly scented white jasmine at the moment.

Wooden shutters graced the windows and the paved courtyard off the main entrance had a gargoyle fountain and a fabulous display of pink camellias in terracotta tubs.

The main rooms were high-ceilinged and perfectly proportioned. Sealed timber floors were scattered with priceless Persian and Chinese rugs. The furniture was a mixture of heirloom and antique, walnut, mahogany, silky oak, and the sheer luxury of modern cushioning in couches and chairs covered in topaz velvet or white brocade.

The lamps, and there were many of them, had a bouquet of deep silk shades in just about every lovely zinnia colour.

The dining-room table seated sixteen and had an exquisite floral inlay.

Behind the scenes, she'd found a large linen press with some of the fine heirloom stuff encrusted with lace appliqués. There were six dinner services to choose from, one of them a very old Spode willow-pattern service that took her back to her childhood—her parents had had one and she'd loved counting the birds and all the other features. There was a vast Community Plate cutlery set in its own cabinet.

Waterford and Stuart crystal glassware abounded. There was enough silverware, including rare pieces like fish forks—from the days when it had been considered a crime to touch fish with steel knives—to keep a butler occupied solely with polishing it.

She'd been allotted a charming bedroom. It had blue and white dotted wallpaper, a double bed beneath a white silk quilt and French Colonial furniture on a powder-blue carpet. She had her own *en suite* bathroom.

But—she hitched her pillows up a bit—there was a slightly neglected air overall. Not so surprising, perhaps, with all the dusting and polishing that was required and after some years without a mistress, only a master, in charge of the house.

She sat up with a sudden frown. Lee Richardson.

No wonder she'd got that impression four years ago that there was more to him than being at home in a boardroom! He not only controlled a vast cattle empire, but he'd also been brought up on cattle stations.

No wonder he was quick-thinking, resourceful and physically powerful.

And, yes, still a compellingly attractive man who'd haunted her dreams for a while but only in a fantasy way, surely? When you'd been dumped by a fiancé upon discovery that you didn't stand to inherit a fortune, when you'd lost the most precious thing you thought you could ever have, the scars were too deep even to think of falling in love again, weren't they?

She grimaced. They certainly had been over the past few years. Apart from a small hiatus when a man she'd shared a taxi with had invaded her imagination, she'd lived like a nun, she'd thought like a nun in so much as no other man had made any impression on her.

Then again, maybe she'd just been too busy, too tied down with responsibilities to live any other kind of life. Which led her to wonder if the scars she'd carried had healed more than she'd realised…

Was that why Lee Richardson had walked back into her life and reawakened some awkward memories rather successfully? Or was it the way he looked at her…?

She swallowed uncomfortably and pleated the coverlet with slender ringless fingers. Then she reminded herself that she was here on a job and no man, however he might embody that sort of aloof, irresistible glamour, was going to stand in her way of doing it.

So she would revert to that nun-like status smartly!

She got up and showered. She pulled a pair of jeans on, a navy blouse and a sky-blue sleeveless quilted jacket—easy to shed when the cool of a morning on the hinterland escarpment warmed up.

There was no one in the kitchen, no sign of life in the house, so she made herself a mug of tea and took it outside to have a look at the gardens.

What met her eyes as she came round the back of the house, or the side the main rooms looked out onto, took her breath away.

Smooth green lawn, a rose garden to die for, a sparkling, grotto-like swimming pool with a shingle-roofed pool house with fluted columns to match the main house, then the ground fell away and the view hit you.

Unobstructed views all the way to the blue Pacific Ocean, rimmed, but looking small and insubstantial in the distance, by the towers of Surfers' Paradise and the Gold Coast. She could even see three hot-air balloons that she appeared to be looking down on.

She was drinking it all in when a voice behind her said, 'Morning, ma'am.'

She turned to see a man in overalls, boots and an old baseball cap carrying a set of baskets and a set of secateurs. He introduced himself as the head gardener, Cliff Reinhardt.

Rhiannon introduced herself and complimented him on his roses. He immediately offered her some for the house as well as some fresh vegetables, and gave her a tour of the garden.

Half an hour later Rhiannon not only had a basket of fresh fruit and vegetables—strawberries, cucumbers, a variety of lettuce, the most mouthwatering-

looking tomatoes, asparagus, aubergines and more—
but she also had enough roses to fill several large vases.

The garden was Cliff's pride and joy and rightly so.
It was three acres, although the whole property took
up fifteen, of sweeping lawns, huge gum trees, secret
walkways and shady nooks. There was a delightful
loggia smothered in port-wine magnolia. There were
beds of agapanthus, lavender, daisies and gardenias as
well as native plants renowned for attracting birds like
grevilleas, melaleucas and kangaroo paw. The hedge-
enclosed herb and vegetable garden was a work of art.

She'd learnt that Cliff sold most of his fruit and
vegetables locally since there was rarely anyone in
residence nowadays, although that looked set to
change.

And she'd learnt that Cliff had been widowed when
his daughter, Christy, was a baby—she was now eleven
going on eighteen, he told Rhiannon, and they lived on
the property.

It was impossible to miss the fact that Cliff
Reinhardt was devoted to the Richardson family.

They were carrying all the bounty to the kitchen
through the stable yard—the stables were also sandstone, two wings with a shingle roof and marvellous
gold and black wrought-iron weather vane—when the
clatter of hooves alerted Rhiannon to the fact that
someone had gone for an early-morning ride.

It proved to be Lee Richardson on a large, spirited
bay and Christy, Cliff's daughter, on a smaller almost
white pony called Poppy.

They reined in and dismounted and a lad emerged
from the stables to take Lee's horse and call the dogs to
order.

Both horses were steaming, both riders looked invigorated and glowing and Christy brought Poppy over to be introduced.

Rhiannon patted the pony and scratched her nose. 'I tell you what, Poppy,' she murmured, as she eyed the arrival expertly, 'you may look as if butter wouldn't melt in your mouth but I wouldn't be surprised if you could talk.'

Christy laughed delightedly, and Poppy, still looking angelic, went to nip Rhiannon on the wrist.

She pulled her arm away in time and Christy scolded the pony in such loving tones, she probably thought she was being praised. Then again it was obvious that the motherless Christy adored her pony.

Rhiannon grimaced; she knew what it was like to be motherless—although not at such a young age. She found herself looking into Lee Richardson's amused eyes.

'You're up and about early,' he said.

He wore jeans, short boots and a navy pullover with military patches. He'd taken off his hard hat and ruffled his dark hair and she'd been right about designer stubble. The blue shadows on his jaw added a definitely sexy aura to his overall aura that was intensely masculine and powerful but marvellously streamlined.

He was the kind of man who took your breath away whether you liked it or not. The kind of man who, through those lazy but all-seeing blue eyes, was probably perfectly aware of the effect he had on you.

Even to the battle you were waging with your better judgement. Not to mention some wayward purely physical responses your body—quite without your permission!—was experiencing.

Rhiannon set her teeth and concentrated for a moment on banishing the insidious little ripples of

sensation that the pure appreciation of the fineness of
Lee Richardson had produced.

Then she said wryly, 'Got a big two days ahead!'
She turned to Cliff. 'Thanks so much for all this. I
promise I'll put it to good use.'

'My pleasure. I'll have some more roses for you
tomorrow but I'll help you carry—'

'It's OK, Cliff,' Lee broke in. 'I'll do it.' And he
hefted the fruit and vegetable baskets leaving
Rhiannon to bring the roses.

The spacious kitchen had windows overlooking the
garden.

It was not only a good place to work, Rhiannon
thought, with its leafy outlook and its pot plants, but
it was also truly pleasant.

They put everything on the box pine table—there was
still no sign of anyone—and Lee went to put the kettle
on.

'What time does the staff start?' she asked with a
frown.

'Eight o'clock or thereabouts.' He consulted his
watch. 'Not for another hour. Sharon—she's chief
cook and bottle-washer—has a school-age kid, which
accounts for her late start, and the variety of cleaners
she is responsible for,' he tipped his hand, 'appear to
please themselves.'

He made himself a cup of instant coffee and came
back to the table to sit down. 'You don't approve?'

One thing she always guarded against was being too
critical so she said only, 'Maybe we could work out a
better system.' She eyed the colourful mounds on the
table. 'But first things first. I need to get these roses
into water. Would you know where the vases are?'

He rubbed his jaw. 'Sadly, no.'

'Oh, well, they must be somewhere.' She started opening cupboards but none held vases.

'Perhaps the cabinets in the dining room?' he suggested. 'You seem to know a bit about horses.'

'I had a couple of cunning, bad-tempered ponies myself.' She smiled and walked through to the dining room, where the cabinets he'd mentioned yielded gold. She brought back four vases, two of them heavy crystal, one of them silver and the last a porcelain urn decorated with birds of paradise.

'I must say,' she commented as she traced the birds with her fingertips, 'your home is literally stuffed with the most glorious array of fine old things.' She looked around for a chopping block and she found a meat mallet and started to crush the stems of the roses and arrange them in the vases. 'I feel,' she looked up and smiled at him, 'like a little girl let loose in a candy store.'

He watched her for a while, how she stood back to study the effect she was achieving, how she blended the colours—pink, yellow, salmon, crimson and cream; how, when she was concentrating, she looped the long side of her hair behind her ear, although it never stayed there. And how expertly she was arranging the roses.

A little different, he reflected, from the swiftly passing but obvious confusion she seemed to have experienced when he'd first spoken to her earlier.

Not such an iron maiden when it comes to men maybe, Ms Fairfax, if you ever were? he thought ironically. But, of course, the irony touches me as well, doesn't it? I put her down as just another woman on the make then I made a resolution *not* to allow myself to be intrigued, but I seem to be growing more interested by the minute…

'My mother and my grandmother were great collectors,' he said at last. 'Did you always have an appreciation of fine old things?'

'I guess so. There.' She moved the vases to a counter. 'I'll work out where to put them shortly. In the meantime I should concentrate on the menu for tomorrow, but,' she looked across at him, 'are you a breakfast person?'

He nodded.

'So am I. I'm starving. How about a herb omelette?' Her fingers hovered over the array of Cliff's fresh herbs.

'That sounds—terrific,' he said gravely.

'And some fresh, proper coffee.' She looked at his mug with disfavour.

'Miss Fairfax, will you marry me?'

She laughed. 'Thank you, sir, but I must respectfully decline.'

'What I don't understand,' Rhiannon said half an hour later when they'd consumed her delicious omelette and she was pouring real perked coffee, 'what I mean to say is—um—great wealth is associated with the Richardson family so…'

'So why do I put up with this state of affairs?' Lee Richardson said with a trace of humour. 'I don't. I don't spend much time here at all these days. The place hasn't really been lived in since my father moved to the south of France. But things have changed now. It seemed sad for it to stand empty with a skeleton staff when Matt and Mary could make it their home.'

Rhiannon nodded without comment.

'I think she does want to learn,' he murmured.

'I'll do my best. Now I really should get busy, Mr Richardson.' She stood up.

'Just a moment.' He frowned. 'What's your background, Rhiannon?'

She shrugged. 'Nothing much.'

'So where did you learn all your—expertise?'

'Here and there.' It was her turn to frown. 'I'm sure your very correct PA checked my business record and my references in case you're wondering whether I'm likely to nick the silver.'

'It's not that.'

Rhiannon sent him a speaking look that said clearly—it had better not be...

He stood up. 'Why so secretive, though?'

'Look, I come and I go. I do my level best to get things running smoothly but I always try to retain a professional...distance, if you like.'

'All the same, you're Luke Fairfax's daughter, aren't you?'

CHAPTER TWO

RHIANNON froze. 'How did you—?' She stopped abruptly.

'How did I know? I didn't until last night. But something about your name niggled me so I looked it up on the internet. I came up with, amongst others, Luke and Reese Fairfax.'

He paused and shrugged. 'They were household names until a few years ago. Two musicians who'd gone into the entrepreneurial side of the business. Their open-air country-music and rock concerts were legendary and made them a lot of money. They had one child, a daughter, Rhiannon, who would be twenty-six now.'

He paused and studied her sudden pallor. 'I'm sorry if this is painful but I believe that your father is still alive, although your mother passed away at the time of the company crash?'

Rhiannon swallowed. 'Yes, but I don't see what it has to do with you.'

He eyed her meditatively. 'I just like to have things right, although—not that it has anything to do with *you*—Richardson's, as a creditor, lost a fair amount of money in the collapse of your father's empire.'

'Now you've really made my day,' Rhiannon said, standing uncharacteristically still. 'So you are concerned about my honesty? In which case, I think it's best if I leave immediately.'

'Oh, no, you don't—'

'You can't stop me,' she flashed at him.

'I could but I won't,' he said coolly. 'Sit down and listen.'

Rhiannon eyed him and couldn't quite suppress a little shiver. He looked so very much the man who always got his way she'd sensed yesterday at the airport and there was no denying his physical presence was impressive, even dressed in jeans and sporting designer stubble—if anything, that made him more impressive.

She forced herself to say, however, 'I'll stand and listen.'

He shrugged. 'I'm not at all concerned about your honesty. It wasn't your father's dishonesty that caused the crash. There were a lot of factors involved. There *were* some bad, rather erratic judgements made but show business is notoriously difficult to predict.' He sat down again and shoved his hands into his pockets. 'Of course, many of the details aren't known.' He looked at her interrogatively.

Rhiannon, rather blindly, went to move away but he got up and propelled her back to her chair. When she hesitated then sat down, he poured them both another cup of coffee and sat down himself.

'I don't suppose the heiress to what was once quite a nice little fortune expected to find herself doing this,' he said.

Rhiannon looked around. 'No, but funnily enough I enjoy it for the most part.'

'So what really did lead to the demise of the family fortune?'

She fiddled with her teaspoon then shrugged. 'I suppose, as a creditor, you're entitled to know.' She paused and frowned. 'How did you become a creditor?'

He stirred his coffee. 'We have a transport division. It started out as a cattle-trucking operation but we expanded into a national express freight carrier. Your father used us to carry all the equipment required for his concerts from venue to venue—sound systems, de-mountable stages and so on.'

Rhiannon closed her eyes briefly. 'I see. Well, it all started to go wrong when my mother was diagnosed with an incurable disease. My father was distraught and that's when he seemed to lose his judgement. He backed the wrong bands, ones that didn't take off, crowds started to fall off, debts mounted, but there was more.'

She stared at her hands. 'He started to play the stock market to help him recoup things but that went pear-shaped. Then, when my mother died, he became acutely depressed.'

Lee Richardson expressed a long, slow breath. 'That would probably account for it.'

She glanced at him then veiled her eyes with her lashes. 'Yes. There was only one course then and that was to go into the hands of the receivers and declare himself bankrupt.'

'How is he now?'

'He's better, he's a lot better, although sometimes he's still crushed by it. But at least he's taken up his music again. He and my aunt, his sister—she's a widow and she lives with us—are both musicians. He's a gui-tarist, she's a pianist and they coach bands, school

bands, music societies and so on. Unfortunately…'
She paused.

'Go on.'

'He's going to need a hip replacement shortly but
we don't have private health cover and there's a
waiting list in the public system. So I'm saving every
cent to get it done privately.'

'I'm sorry,' Lee Richardson said. 'It must be quite
a load to carry.'

Rhiannon's head drooped briefly then she squared
her shoulders and tilted her chin. 'I'll cope.'

'How about financially? Are you the only breadwin-
ner in the family now?'

'More or less. He gets a pension and Di, my aunt,
gives piano lessons but it's…' She stopped and started
again. 'Now that I've made a go of this business, it's
a lot easier. Funnily enough, that day…' She stopped.

'Tell me,' he invited.

'That day we shared a taxi was the day I got my first
job doing this kind of thing. Oh, on a much smaller
scale, but it was a start. And the reason I was in such a
rush was to get home, because I'd had to leave my father
on his own to go to the interview. Of course, that was four
years ago, when I was still really worried about him.'

He studied her averted cheek and the way her
fingers were plaited around her coffee-cup, but she
moved suddenly then jumped up, saying, 'All of which
reminds me that I came here to do a job so I'd better
get on with it.'

She hesitated then turned to look at him. 'Unless—
if you don't feel you want to employ me because of
what happened. I would understand.'

Lee Richardson stretched his long legs out. 'Do I
look like a monster?'

'No.' She coloured. 'But it's a rather difficult position to be in. I just thought—'

'Well, don't,' he recommended.

'OK,' she said slowly. 'Thanks. And now I'd just like to establish a couple of things before I get to work. Where are the nearest shops, how will I get to them, do you have a credit system or do I need cash? Oh, and what about the bar tomorrow night? Do you need me to organise wine, spirits or whatever?'

'You can leave the bar to me, we're extensively stocked anyway.' Lee stood up. 'But I'll leave soft drinks to you.' He pulled a set of car keys from his pocket and handed them to her. 'You can use the blue Mercedes station wagon in the garage. Mount Tamborine is our nearest village and you can put anything you buy on Southall's tab. I'll give you a note of introduction and draw you some directions.'

Half an hour later, Rhiannon parked the wagon and got out to enjoy the sights and sounds of Mount Tamborine.

It was not only a pretty village with lovely trees and gardens, but there were also art galleries, craft shops and interesting-looking restaurants. Several large buses alerted her to the fact that it was on a scenic tourist route and the clear mountain air was lovely.

When she got back to Southall, it was to notice a yellow Lamborghini parked in the driveway.

She raised her eyebrows but thought no more about it because by this time Sharon, the housekeeper, had started work.

Sharon was six feet tall, in her middle thirties and friendly.

'Thank heavens someone is here to—well,' she said to Rhiannon, then looked embarrassed, 'I wasn't sure if the party was still on after the shenanigans of yesterday, not to mention this morning—damn! I wasn't going to say anything about that.' She reddened.

'It's OK, I'm up-to-date,' Rhiannon assured her, 'and the party is still on.' She stopped, struck by a sudden thought. 'You wouldn't know who the guests are, would you?'

'Not by name but they're all Mary's friends from TV and the movies. Some of them are flying in from interstate apparently—oh, not to stay here but down on the coast.'

Rhiannon stared at her. 'She must have been really upset to walk out—I mean—'

'She was. She doesn't like living up here and Matt has been away for a week on business so she was feeling extra-lonely and she's...' Sharon grimaced. 'Don't get me wrong, there's a lot to like about her but she can be a bit spoilt. She's so gorgeous, she's probably used to getting her own way a lot.'

'I see.'

'Oh, by the way, she told me she'd organised a DJ, hopefully for the right date, but I'm not sure if Lee knows about it. And it may be more than thirty people, she told me she'd lost count but she thought it could be forty or fifty. She has a lot of friends.'

Rhiannon heaved a sigh. 'I think I'd better tell him.'

But, along the way, Rhiannon got another surprise.

She almost bumped into a strange woman who was striding through the lounge, probably the most beautiful woman she'd ever seen.

For a moment she wondered if it was Mary

Richardson then decided not; this woman was in her early thirties, possibly, and she looked faintly familiar. She also, from her flashing dark eyes, set mouth and the way she was walking, looked furious…

'Oh, sorry! Hello,' Rhiannon said, and introduced herself.

'Ah, the housekeeper! How do you do? I'm Andrea Richardson.'

Rhiannon blinked. 'You mean…?' She broke off as full recognition dawned.

Andrea Richardson née Comero was tall and had a river of dark, glossy hair flowing down her back. Her skin was smooth and olive, her lips a luscious red, and she wore a glorious pomegranate-pink silk blouse with hipster black satin trousers and silver sandals. She held herself regally and you could just see her striding the catwalk…

'The wicked stepmother no less?' Andrea shot back. 'Yes, that's me.'

'I—didn't mean that at all,' Rhiannon disclaimed. 'I mean to say, all I know is that you married Ross Richardson but most people probably know that.' She looked quizzical for a moment.

'Then you either haven't been here long enough to hear otherwise or they've been unusually discreet.' Andrea Richardson shook out her hair. 'They—make that particularly Lee—regard me as a fortune huntress who preyed upon their father and trampled the sacred memory of their mother.'

Rhiannon stared at her with her lips parted. 'I—uh—I don't know anything about that. Anyway, it has nothing to do with me, I'm just here to do a job.'

'Well, don't be surprised if you're shortly taking your orders from *me*, Miss Fairfax. Please do excuse me now.'

And she stalked away with a hip-swinging walk that contrived to be provocative even though it was so angry.

Rhiannon found Lee Richardson in the library.

She looked longingly at the book-lined walls for a moment then advanced across the red Turkish rug towards the desk. French windows opened on to a side-veranda and the perfume of jasmine wafted in. One end of the room held a comfortable settee and armchair covered in mint-green crushed velvet, as well as a writing table.

The desk at the other end of the room, where Lee was working, was much bigger and held some impressive computer equipment.

She stopped in front of it and sniffed. There was another perfume on the air and overlaying the jasmine. A perfume she knew because she had used to wear it herself. The same perfume Andrea Richardson had been wearing, now she came to think of it.

So, putting two and two together, had an angry confrontation between Lee and Andrea Richardson just taken place in the library? One could be forgiven for thinking so, Rhiannon reasoned and suddenly remembered Sharon's comments about the shenanigans of yesterday, not to mention this morning…

She decided the matter in the affirmative when Lee looked up.

He did not look to be in a good mood. His eyes were hard, his face was set in uncompromising lines.

'Mr Richardson, I'm sorry to disturb you—'

'Call me Lee, Rhiannon, and have a seat. You look like the bearer of ill-tidings. Don't tell me your confidence of yesterday at the airport was misplaced?'

It had happened to her before and it happened to her

again. One moment she found herself feeling—how to put it?—in charity with this man, the next, he said or did something that made her feel as if she'd had a door slammed in her face. But that was ridiculous she assured herself angrily, and sat down.

'I've just been given to understand that a conflict of interest may have arisen,' she said precisely

He frowned. 'What on earth are you talking about?'

'I've just met your—stepmother. She led me to believe she might be the one to be in charge.'

She saw his teeth clench and a look of supreme irritation chase through his eyes but he only said one word, a lethally cold one, all the same. 'No.'

'But—'

'Rhiannon,' he overrode her, 'what I say goes and that's all there is to it.'

'But if she lives here it could make things awkward for me, I mean—'

'She does not live here.'

'Well, if you're sure—' She broke off and bit her lip as he swore softly. 'OK. Um—what you obviously believed was going to be a...refined buffet dinner for thirty people may not be that at all and not only number-wise.' And she passed on Sharon's news, including the DJ.

'Bloody hell!' Lee Richardson swore quite audibly this time.

'That may not be such a bad idea,' Rhiannon murmured. 'To keep them entertained.'

He stared at her broodingly.

'I believe she's only twenty-two, your sister-in-law,' Rhiannon said.

'That's—what? A whole four years younger than you?'

Rhiannon shrugged. 'She can't help it if she hasn't had some tough times yet. She also,' she hesitated, 'well, apparently she doesn't like it up here.' She stopped awkwardly.

'Go on.'

'No, it's nothing to do with me. Look, I've really got an awful lot to—'

'You wondered what she's doing stuck up here?'

'Well, yes,' Rhiannon confessed.

'It suits me to have someone legitimate in residence,' he said thoughtfully. 'And, since you're bound to work this out for yourself, Mary and my brother need something real to settle them into marriage rather than the erratic course Mary had in mind.'

'Erratic?' Rhiannon stared at him.

'She wanted to live in Brisbane or on the coast and continue her career.'

'I hesitate to say this but most women have that ambition in regard to their careers these days.'

They exchanged glances, hers combative, his amused.

He said, 'Before you label me a male chauvinist, I agree that's the way it is these days but—'

'You don't have to approve, you were going to say?' she interrupted tartly. 'That's almost the same thing.'

'Don't put words into my mouth, Rhiannon,' he advised coolly. 'I was going to say that, if Mary had wanted to continue her career and her particular lifestyle, she should have at least taken into consideration Matt's side of the story before she married him.'

'Which is?' Rhiannon raised a cool eyebrow at him.

'A lot of responsibility and a heavy workload.'

'Could he not handle that from a milieu she's more at home in, though?' Rhiannon queried.

'Yes, possibly he could, but after he's taken *six months* off to take her around the world on an extended, expensive honeymoon by anyone's standards, wouldn't you consider that some time spent living where *he wants* to live and showing some interest in the Richardson side of things would be appropriate?'

Rhiannon rubbed the bridge of her nose.

'She is also pregnant,' he murmured.

Rhiannon heaved a sigh. 'Maybe you're right—in theory. But theories don't always work with living, breathing people and I'm just relieved—' she smiled ruefully '—it's not my problem.' She gestured a little helplessly.

'You wouldn't have that problem yourself?'

She frowned. 'What problem?'

'You wouldn't find living at Southall a penance?'

'A *penance*?' She looked at him as if he were mad. 'The opposite, if anything.' She stood up. 'Be that as it may, about the party.'

He sat up. 'Yes. About the party. I'm sure your thoughts on the subject are invaluable, Rhiannon.'

She grimaced, then reminded herself she had a job to do, and do it to the best of her ability she would.

'Well, I've got the food under control. Most of it can be prepared this afternoon, so it only needs heating up tomorrow. But rather than using the dining room I suggest we use the east veranda. It's big enough to dance on and house the DJ.'

'True. We also have some standard gas heaters to warm it up if necessary.'

'Oh, good! And Sharon has told me she's got two extra pairs of hands for tomorrow to help in the kitchen. But what may be a problem with so many people is the lack of waiters. I haven't worked out how to handle that.'

'Uh—Cliff used to double as a waiter sometimes for my mother. He also used to set things up, tables and so on, for outside parties. I'm sure he'd be happy to do the same for you. And he has a friend he used to rope in—I'll organise that. As a matter of fact, I agree to it all on one condition.'

'What's that?' She looked at him abstractedly, her mind on the million things she had to do.

'That you come to the party as a guest rather than lurking behind the scenes.'

This time she not only looked it but also said it as her gaze snapped back into focus. 'You must be mad!'

He shook his head.

'I won't have a moment to spare!'

'You will have staff,' he pointed out. 'You've just told me about Sharon's arrangements and that most of the cooking will be done earlier.'

'Mr Richardson—Lee, I don't want to do this!'

He shrugged. 'Then we'll call it off.'

'The party?'

'What else?' he enquired drily.

She stared at him, totally nonplussed and with the distinct impression she'd run into a brick wall. It also caused her to wonder how secure the rest of this assignment would be if she tried to dig in her heels but she made one last despairing effort.

'I don't have anything to wear!'

'Thus work the minds of women,' he murmured and Rhiannon could have killed herself for making such a feeble objection. 'I'm sure Mary could help out,' he added.

'No, don't do that! I…this…*why*?' she asked intently.

'I feel your influence will be better exerted from the front line rather than behind the scenes.'

'You make *me* feel like a sergeant major!' she said resentfully.

'Ah, but much better looking,' he said. 'No, don't take it the wrong way. It is part of your job description, after all.' He paused and summed her up from head to toe.

She'd discarded her blue waistcoat and she looked young and slim but capable and brimming with vitality. You just knew, he reflected, that you were in good hands even if she stayed behind the scenes tomorrow night. So why was he doing this?

'Scared, Rhiannon?' he asked as the answer to his question articulated itself, or started to.

'Scared? What do you mean?' She looked baffled.

'That you might not be able to maintain your absolute indifference to me in a partying mode?'

The colour started at the base of her throat. She clenched her fists but it mounted all the same to stain her cheeks pink. She pushed her hair behind her ear almost savagely but her cheeks still burned and she appeared to be lost for words.

'I just wondered, you see,' he continued softly, 'if we didn't strike sparks off each other when we first met this morning. Well, amend that.' The ghost of a smile touched his eyes. 'I know you struck a certain chord with me.'

Rhiannon felt herself go from hot to cold then back again. She swallowed. She knew that never in a million years would she admit to the undoubted *frisson* he'd produced in her this morning.

But denying it could be another matter. Would he believe her? Had she given herself away in those few moments of confusion? She'd certainly got the feeling at the time that she had. How had it happened to her anyway? It was *four years* ago since she'd first been affected by this man.

'Ms Fairfax?' He interrupted her chaotic thoughts gravely.

She took hold and swept him with a look of scorn out of her sparkling brown eyes that was meant to tell him she had no intention of playing word games—or cat-and-mouse games, come to that—with him. She would simply ignore the issue.

'Well, it's up to you,' she said coolly and shrugged as if it was all a storm in a teacup anyway. 'You're the boss. Now I really do need to get to work.'

She swung on her heel and marched towards the door.

'Isn't that a little less than honest and upfront, Rhiannon?' he queried.

She stopped and, after a moment, turned back.

'Mr Richardson, I don't care what men think of me, with good reason, believe me. So if you want to change your mind, you're welcome to; it really doesn't matter one way or the other to me.'

Their gazes clashed and held, his was entirely inscrutable, hers was defiant.

'No, I won't change my mind.' That inscrutable gaze skimmed her figure and he added, 'I don't mind jeans on women in general but on you it's criminal to hide such a marvellous pair of legs.'

She took a sharp breath. 'You're wasting your time, you know,' she warned through her teeth.

'I'll reserve judgement on that. Please don't let me detain you, Rhiannon.' He raised his eyebrows. 'Especially since—if looks could kill I'd be six feet under now.'

'I wish you were!' she retorted then bit her lip and stalked out of the room.

Lee Richardson watched her go with a quizzical expression. Then he sobered and once again asked himself what on earth he thought he was doing.

CHAPTER THREE

'"FOOD, glorious food!"' Sharon sang from the musical *Oliver* in a clear, high soprano.

She was an enthusiastic member of the local operatic society, Rhiannon had learnt in the hours they'd worked together.

She also put her height and lean, rangy build to good use on the basketball court.

And she was nice. Sharon confessed to Rhiannon that she desperately needed the kind of input Margaret Richardson had given her now Southall was to be lived in again.

'She always knew what to serve, she always did the flowers herself and decorated the tables, and the cleaning staff *really* cleaned while she was around. I don't seem to have the same effect on them and neither does Mary,' she'd confided ruefully to Rhiannon.

Rhiannon had told her warmly that she'd done a great job nevertheless. And she'd opened her mouth to ask Sharon about Andrea Richardson, who seemed to have disappeared along with the yellow Lamborghini, but changed her mind.

Then they'd started talking food, found they were kindred spirits and they'd set to work in great harmony.

Sharon had dug out six big copper-based silver-lidded food warmers that operated on spirit lamps set into the base below them. They were old-fashioned perhaps but effective and stylish.

What had prompted Sharon to burst into song was the fact that their efforts were all but complete and a marvellous array of dishes stood on counters and the kitchen table, all set to be refrigerated overnight when they'd cooled down then warmed in the copper-based servers tomorrow.

From a previous job in the state, Rhiannon had discovered that Queenslanders really loved their seafood, and there was an abundance of it to choose from. The local shops had yielded a bonanza.

Rhiannon had made a seafood casserole containing crab and Moreton Bay bug meat with fresh asparagus in a cream, herb and brandy sauce that smelled divine, and tomorrow she intended to assemble platters heaped with fresh peeled prawns and oysters, with bowls of lemon wedges and tangy dipping sauces.

There were two large legs of ham that had been scored and pricked with cloves, all set to be basted with brown sugar and pineapple juice as they cooked tomorrow.

Sharon had cooked three different rice dishes that only needed to be heated up in the microwave to be fluffy and perfect. She'd also concocted a chicken and Marsala casserole, as well as a beef and black-bean sauce one with Asian crisp vegetables. Rhiannon had made a potato frittata and tomorrow she would put Cliff's fresh produce to good use as promised in a cauliflower *au gratin* dish, several salads and a ratatouille.

And between them they'd baked four pavlovas to be heaped with strawberries and served with cream and ice cream for dessert.

'There.' Rhiannon stood back and looped her hair behind her ear. 'Most of it only needs to be heated up just before you set it out, then we can keep it warm in the servers. Really, apart from the prawns and the vegetable and salad dishes, all that needs to be done just before time is the fried chicken legs so they're nice and crispy, and carving the ham as well as buttering the rolls. We've done well!' she added with a grin at Sharon.

She'd already explained to Sharon that she wouldn't be much help in the kitchen but she'd pop in as frequently as she could.

'We sure have. Just one thing—what about snacks?' Sharon replied. 'Peanuts and so on.'

'No snacks,' Rhiannon said. 'It's so easy to fill up on nuts and things so that you're not hungry for anything else that will soak up…' She paused.

'The alcohol? Too true.' Sharon agreed.

'OK.' Rhiannon untied her apron and glanced at her watch. It was five o'clock. 'Thanks, Sharon. Off you go and have a pleasant evening! I'll see you tomorrow—don't worry about being early, it's going to be a long day. Who looks after your child, incidentally, when you're working?'

'My mother, so it's no problem. Um—are you going to cook Lee's dinner? He's a big steak fan and—'

'Actually, Lee has other ideas,' Lee himself said as he strolled into the kitchen, 'but I just wanted to give you this, Sharon, a small token of my appreciation of all your efforts, plus a little something for your mum.' He slipped an envelope into Sharon's hand.

'Oh, you didn't have to do that!' Sharon looked all flustered.

'Yes I did.' He closed her hand over the envelope then gave her a little push towards the back door.

'That was nice of you,' Rhiannon approved once the door had closed on Sharon. 'I would definitely recommend keeping her on. So, I take it you're going out and don't need dinner here?'

'We are going out.'

'We? Who's we?'

He looked around quizzically. 'There's only you and me left, Rhiannon, so it has to be us.'

'But I don't want to go out and you haven't asked me!' she protested.

'Then I'll ask you now, not that I intend to take no for an answer. Come and have dinner with me in the village, Ms Fairfax. For one good reason, I can't imagine anyone who's done as much cooking as you have today being remotely interested in more; and for another, I'd like to be assured you don't still wish me dead.'

Rhiannon ground her teeth. 'I didn't say that.'

'Wishing I were six feet under has to be the same thing,' he said gravely.

'You were the one…' She broke off. 'All right, I may have—'

'You did.'

'I didn't really mean it. Satisfied?' She eyed him.

'Not unless you have dinner with me.' He'd propped himself against a kitchen counter with his arms folded.

He'd changed into khaki trousers and a long-sleeved, light blue linen shirt. He looked big, relaxed yet entirely immoveable.

Rhiannon made a kittenish little sound of frustration.

He straightened, went to the fridge and brought out a bottle of wine. He poured a glass and handed it to her.

'Go and have a soak in a warm bath, wash your hair

and whatever else girls do. The restaurant I have in mind is informal but pleasant and the food's good. We'll leave at six-thirty—no, don't say no or I'll come and help you.'

She tossed him such a sparkling look of outrage, he laughed softly and said, 'On the other hand, I've had my shower and changed.'

'I never thought you actually meant it!'

'I wouldn't put it to the test, shower or no shower, Rhiannon. And I wouldn't be too sure you wouldn't enjoy it, either.'

Their gazes clashed but, although his was still amused, she'd had at least two demonstrations of the lengths Lee Richardson would go to to get his own way today.

Not only that but she was also afflicted by a sudden vision of them showering together, of him soaping her body and…

She switched her mental vision off with an audible click, audible only to her. But her heels did click on the kitchen tiles as she turned away from him and swept out.

It was when she was spraying on her perfume, a precious bottle given to her for Christmas by her aunt, that Andrea Richardson came back to mind suddenly.

She'd done everything Lee had suggested—soaked in the bath, washed her hair and changed her clothes for taupe linen trousers and a lime-green silky knit top cinched into her waist with a wide bronze belt.

But she couldn't help wondering suddenly what place Ross Richardson's widow held in the family now. Obviously not a happy one but surely she deserved some status?

She shrugged, checked her reflection and took a deep breath.

'Not such a bad idea after all,' Lee said to her over a red and white checked tablecloth and an oil lamp on the restaurant veranda.

'No,' Rhiannon had to agree.

She'd managed to put her somewhat tortured animosity towards this man on hold but she had to admit he'd helped by being strictly companionable in a non-threatening way.

And, true to Sharon's prediction, he'd tackled a large steak while she had made a much smaller meal of whiting fillets but enjoyed it.

She smiled, albeit a little reluctantly. 'The amazing thing is that I was actually hungry.'

'It must be a problem for a passionate cook, a soupçon here and there too many.'

'Yes,' she fingered her wine glass delicately, 'you need to be strong-willed.'

'I believe you are, Rhiannon, and not only when it comes to cooking.'

'Probably. It may also take one to know one.'

He raised a dark eyebrow at her. 'Are we trading insults again?'

She raised her glass and sipped her wine as she looked at him through her lashes. 'I don't know. Are we?'

He smiled, that sudden, unexpected smile that wreaked so much havoc. 'Oh, I think so. I think we rather enjoy it. But war has its other side.'

'Not in my case,' she denied.

'Liar,' he accused softly and sat back.

She found herself studying the tanned line of his

throat revealed by the V-neck of his shirt before she switched her gaze away abruptly. 'Can we talk about something else?'

'Sure.' He shrugged those broad, tantalising shoulders. 'You choose.'

She hesitated, then, 'Tell me about your lifestyle.'

'Well, it's changed a bit since I took over from my father. I used to spend a lot more time outback—that was the area I concentrated on, but I make a lot of decisions from a boardroom these days. Have you,' he paused and frowned fleetingly, 'any position on an outback lifestyle?'

Rhiannon looked startled. 'Cattle stations? I once spent a wonderful holiday on a cattle station called Beaufort, in the Kimberley. It's owned and operated by the Constantin family. I had a ball!'

'I know it,' he said. 'Tatiana and Alex Constantin are friends. Of course, he's into pearls in a big way as well as cattle.'

'Yes.' Rhiannon grimaced. 'My parents gave me a string of their South Sea Pearls for my eighteenth birthday. They were stunning but I had to sell them. That was hard,' she said ruefully, 'but I did really enjoy the whole outback experience. Of course, it helps if you ride and I do— What's wrong?' she added when she suddenly realised he was studying her rather intently.

'So you don't find cattle stations dusty and boring?'

'Good heavens, no! Mind you, the Kimberley is unique but—why do you ask?'

He took in the genuine enthusiasm in her eyes. 'No reason. Mary is not a fan.'

Rhiannon rubbed the bridge of her nose, then she said with a wry little chuckle, 'To be honest, I can't help feeling a little sorry for Mary even though I've never met her. She seems to be up against some rather large odds.'

'Oh, I think Mary can look after herself in her own way. Incidentally, what exactly did my stepmother say to you today?'

Rhiannon hesitated and thought about declining to be drawn on the subject but she intercepted a narrowed, determined look from Lee Richardson she was learning not to take lightly.

'She—well, she was obviously in a bit of a temper but the gist of it was that you, particularly, regard her as the wicked stepmother who trapped your father into marriage.' Rhiannon looked uncomfortable.

'But that's not all?' he said.

'She did—I think—look, it's got nothing to do with me,' she gestured, 'but maybe she feels she's entitled to some place at Southall?'

He said nothing, merely stared over her shoulder with his eyes focused on the distance.

Rhiannon drained her wine, fought a small battle with herself, but curiosity got the better of her. 'What—does she do these days?'

He withdrew his gaze from the distance and it was intensely blue as it rested on her face. 'When she's not making mischief? Not much. She flits between the south of France and Australia, but she does believe that Southall should be her home.'

Rhiannon frowned. 'What kind of mischief? And does she have any basis to believe that?'

'She's rather enslaved Mary for her own ends and there's a slightly awkward clause in my father's will, granting her residence under certain conditions.'

'When you say she's enslaved Mary, what do you mean?'

'She's preyed on Mary's desire to blend her old life with her new one; she's egging her on, in other words, to persuade Matt to move to Brisbane. Other than that,' he shrugged, 'at present, she's conceived the idea of a memorial service for my father around the anniversary of his death.'

'Do you regard her—I mean, *do* you resent her marriage to your father?' Rhiannon asked.

'Wouldn't you in the circumstances? She was half his age, my mother hadn't been gone that long and she contrived to marry him without Matt or me knowing what was going on.'

Rhiannon blinked, then blinked again. 'It sounds,' she grimaced, 'tricky.'

'No, it's not tricky at all,' he disagreed and the coldest gleam of blue fire lit his eyes for a moment, causing Rhiannon to shiver inwardly.

Then it was gone and he said, 'Well, I guess you wouldn't mind an early night?'

Rhiannon glanced at her watch to see that it was nine o'clock. The time had gone fast. She said, 'You presume right but thanks for dinner—it was probably just what I needed.'

They drove through the wrought-iron gates but Lee slammed on the brakes before they reached the garage.

'Did you see that?' he snapped.

'What? No, I didn't see anything—hang on,' she paused as a shrill whinny tore the air, accompanied by pounding hooves, 'it's a loose horse by the sound of it.'

'It's not a horse, it's that blasted she-devil of Christy's impersonating one—she's got out somehow.'

'Poppy! But how?' Rhiannon stopped abruptly as a chorus of barks rent the air.

'She's the ultimate escape artist and the dogs are chasing her. They're all having a fine game, no doubt,' Lee said grimly.

'But what about the stable lad and Christy and Cliff? Wouldn't they—?'

'The stable lad goes home at night, the dogs are supposed to be patrolling the place and Cliff and Christy go to the club every Saturday night. It's the night they run chess and Scrabble competitions.' He got out and slammed the car door and started to whistle.

Two highly excited dogs, the ones she'd seen that morning, streaked through the night towards him, grinning all over their faces.

'Sit,' he commanded.

They obliged smartly.

'You're safe, Rhiannon,' Lee called. 'They're trained not to attack. OK, guys,' he added to the dogs, 'heel! We'll get you shut up then—Rhiannon, would you mind giving me a hand? Poppy can also be the ultimate vandal when she sets her mind to it. She can actually turn on taps with her teeth.'

'Certainly.' Rhiannon stepped out of the car. 'I wouldn't be surprised if she's in the vegetable garden as we speak.'

'Whow! *Having* turned on a few taps, on the way,' he cursed as he stepped into a large puddle that shouldn't have been there. 'I don't know why I put up with this blasted horse!'

'Because you're rather fond of Christy?' Rhiannon suggested with a smile.

They discovered how Poppy had got out when they reached the stables. She'd kicked a hole in the lower half of her stall door and somehow scrambled through.

'You have to give her some marks for sheer inge-
nuity,' Rhiannon laughed, although Lee was swearing
as he locked up the dogs.

'OK, let's arm ourselves.' He took down two leads
and a headstall from hooks on the wall and gathered
two biscuits of lucerne hay from the feed room.

As Rhiannon had predicted, they found Poppy in the
vegetable garden—where she'd turned on another tap
thereby creating something of a quagmire—expertly
digging up carrots.

'Oh, poor Cliff,' Rhiannon breathed as she summed
up the devastation in the moonlight.

'It might just prompt him to consider getting his
daughter a decent, well-mannered horse,' Lee said
caustically. 'Let's back her into that corner.' He
pointed. 'I don't think she can get through that hedge.
Oh, Poppy,' he called in dulcet, singsong tones as he
advanced with his lucerne, 'if you know what's good
for you, you old witch, you'll come quietly!'

Poppy had other ideas, but with two experienced
horsemen in front of her and a thick, scratchy hedge
behind her, she was finally cornered, although Lee
caught his shirt in the hedge, ripping it severely and
finally abandoning it on a wicked thorn.

Neither of them said a word as they marched the
pony back to the stables, nor as Lee put her into the
sand-roll and closed the metal door on her, but it wasn't
a silent time. The dogs were barking; the other horses
were all stirred up.

They checked them out individually and mixed
some small feeds to settle them all down.

Then they stood in the middle of the stable yard and
eyed each other.

Rhiannon was the first to crack. 'Talk about a snow

man—you look like a mud man!' she gurgled. 'It's in your hair, all over your chest, everywhere.'

'I know that,' he countered. 'And talk about a mud maiden—you look as if you've gone through some bizarre tribal ritual. There's only one thing to do.' He shrugged. 'What does a little more water matter anyway?'

He reached for the stable hose, turned it on and sprayed himself from head to toe.

'Your turn now!'

She couldn't stop laughing long enough to tell him not to—and it was the only sensible thing to do anyway, so she accepted her hosing down.

But something changed between them, an awareness grew between them out of nowhere.

She was struck by the beautiful proportions of his upper body, clean and slick now. She could only drink in the width of his sleekly muscled shoulders, his taut diaphragm, his lean waist and the mat of dark hair disappearing into the waistband of his trousers...

'You look like a siren,' he said huskily, causing her to look up guiltily.

'A well-dressed one.' She glanced down at herself and bit her lip. Her top was moulded to her breasts, her nipples clearly outlined, so were her thighs.

'Maybe not so well-dressed,' he murmured.

Her eyes flew to his. 'No, I mean—'

'Yes,' he said softly. 'Luscious and very lovely.'

She started to colour. His eyes glinted wickedly.

Rhiannon clenched her fists. She battled to control the tremors that were starting to run through her as that dark blue gaze of his swept her body again—it was almost as if there was an electric current running between them.

The moonlit stable yard with its puddles of water, the sounds of munching, now contented horses, all had a surreal quality and for a blinding moment she wished she were young and refreshingly open again. So that she could reach that open, honest plane with Lee Richardson...

If he made one step forward, she thought, she'd be lost. She'd be vulnerable to all those fantasies about him she'd thought, wrongly, she'd banished.

She'd be as helpless—no!

'I think it might be timely to remember,' she said with an effort, 'that basically, I'm the housekeeper here on a job. Goodnight.'

She swung on her heel and squelched through the yard towards the kitchen door.

Lee made no attempt to follow her, although he stared after her with a muscle flickering in his jaw.

She saw little of him the next morning and was grateful for all the work she had to do towards the party—it was one way of keeping her thoughts on other things at bay. It hadn't been an easy night...

Not only that, but there was also a devastated Cliff to counsel and a subdued Christy to handle.

'One more incident like that and she has to go,' Christy told her tearfully. 'Not only is Lee mad but so's my father. She trampled his prize begonias and his vegetable garden is wrecked.'

'I know,' Rhiannon said ruefully.

'Actually, I've never seen Lee in such a bad mood,' Christy confided.

Rhiannon paused and grimaced inwardly. 'Well, I wouldn't be surprised if they get over it, both Lee and your dad. But in the meantime it would be a good idea to be firmer with Poppy, Christy. Don't let her get away with murder. If I had more time I'd help you. Maybe after the party I'll be able to sort something out.'

Christy went away looking happier.

But Rhiannon still had the girl on her mind when she did bump into Lee and it led to a tense little encounter.

She was sorting cutlery and wrapping each knife and fork in a linen napkin on the dining-room sideboard when he walked through the room on his way to the kitchen.

'Ah. Basically the housekeeper,' he said sardonically, coming to a stop beside her.

She flicked him a quick glance and went on wrapping cutlery. 'Good afternoon.'

'How is your day going so far, Ms Fairfax?' he enquired.

'As well as can be expected, Mr Richardson. How's yours?'

'Not without its complications. Things would appear to be a little tense.'

'Just don't take it out on Christy!' she flashed at him then could have shot herself.

He opened his mouth, closed it and said smoothly, 'What would you recommend? That I give her a certificate? Pretend Poppy's escapades were laudable?'

Rhiannon set her teeth. 'No. But don't transfer any annoyance you might be feeling towards me onto her.'

'Now, what on earth made you think that?' he drawled.

'Men can have fragile egos,' she retorted. 'And, since I got myself into this impossible conversation, I might as well keep going. Someone needs to give Christy some help with Poppy, so why don't you?'

He put his head to one side. 'You really are the most complete housekeeper, aren't you?' he said, annoyed. 'Will there be any aspect of our lives you haven't reorganised by the time you leave?'

'She is only eleven, she doesn't have a mother, she *loves* Poppy—any one of you could have worked that out, I would have thought.'

'Are you suggesting I become a horse whisperer in my spare time?'

'Yes.'

He regarded her bent head and busy fingers thoughtfully. 'Since you're such a fountain of wisdom, Rhiannon, how would you suggest I deal with a difficult night filled with visions of you, clothed but soaking wet then *unclothed* in my arms?' He waited then went on,

'Or, since you're so touchy this afternoon,' he paused as she lifted her head and their gazes clashed, 'maybe you had a similar night? In which case, perhaps you could tell me what the hell we're fighting about.'

Her throat worked but nothing came out.

He smiled drily and walked away but they both stopped what they were doing, she folding napkins and he turning back, and they spoke simultaneously.

'Look,' he said.

'Listen,' Rhiannon said.

The silence grew after their words had clashed until he said, 'Be my guest.'

'I think we should—put aside all this,' she said with an effort. 'It's going to be a huge day one way or another and…' She gestured helplessly.

'My sentiments entirely. Should we sign an *entente cordiale* for today at least?'

'I think we should agree to one, anyway. And,' she frowned, 'talking of guests, are you still sure you want me as one? It really would be much easier—'

'I'm afraid to say on that point I'm rocksolid,' he murmured. 'I see you as invaluable on the social scene.'

She blinked. 'But why?'

'You're very talented, Rhiannon. It just,' he shrugged, 'shines through. As a matter of fact, you remind me of my mother. She managed to blend considerable social skills with a streak of solid-gold practicality and genuine warmth.'

'But,' Rhiannon objected frustratedly, 'that's Mary's role!'

He shrugged again. 'One day, maybe. It hasn't yet happened. So that's signed and sealed?'

She stared at him. 'Well…'

He smiled at her, the hundred-and-fifty-watt version.

'Oh, all right!' She turned away hastily and went back to wrapping cutlery.

Two hours before the guests arrived Rhiannon was happy with all her preparations, and she decided to take a break, checking up on the veranda, where Cliff was setting things up, on her way out for a breath of fresh air.

Three long trestle tables clothed in dark green linen had been set up for the food and a portable bar was tucked into a corner. Smaller round tables and chairs were scattered about as well as some potted lemon trees.

Candle glasses sat on the tables and lined the edge of the veranda. A bowl of roses and a lovely silver six-branch candelabrum with pink candles dominated the main table.

She moved the roses and the candelabrum to show them off more effectively and repositioned the baskets of linen-wrapped cutlery and stood back to study the effect.

Satisfied, she looked at the sky but it was clear and there was no breeze.

'Good night for it, thank heavens!' she said to Cliff who was working behind the bar.

'Not only that, we've got a full moon tonight. It's quite a sight from up here,' he replied.

Rhiannon looked enchanted. 'I believe you!'

She decided to enjoy the rose garden for a few minutes before she went indoors again. The sun was starting to set. A flock of corellas, white parrots without the sulphur crests of cockatoos, was wheeling and squawking as they made the best of the last of the daylight before they put themselves to bed.

There was a sprinkler system watering a section of the garden and lawn and raising the rich scent of damp earth and wet grass.

She stopped and breathed in deeply—it really was the most beautiful place and it brought back memories of her home before the crash. Although it hadn't been as grand as Southall, her parents had had a lovely estate perched in the Blue Mountains above Sydney.

She sniffed suddenly as she thought of it, and her father and mother.

Tears trickled down her cheeks.

She brushed them away with her fingers and turned to go in, only to bump into Lee Richardson.

He put out a hand to steady her. 'Rhiannon?' He frowned down at her. 'What's wrong?'

'Nothing.' She pulled a hanky from her pocket and blew her nose. 'Some pollen, maybe, that's all.'

He looked unconvinced and she rushed into speech, the first thing that came to mind.

'What on earth have you been doing?'

He looked down at his sweat-soaked T-shirt, track pants and bare feet. He also had a towel slung round his neck. 'Boxing.'

Her lips parted in surprise. 'You're a—boxer?'

He raised an eyebrow. 'What's wrong with that?'

'It's a horrible sport!'

'There you go, making snap judgements again,' he drawled. 'Done scientifically and with all the proper rules, it's actually a great way for boys to let off steam and curb their sometimes naturally destructive instincts—as I should know. Walk with me,' he added. 'I'm going for a swim.'

She hesitated then fell into step beside him. 'What do you mean? And who have you been *fighting*?'

He laughed. 'A bunch of late-teen boys at a sports club the family set up and endowed some years ago. I always try to show my face when I'm here.'

Rhiannon blinked a couple of times. 'That—sounds rather laudable if only it wasn't boxing. And why should you know about boys needing to let off steam et cetera?'

They'd reached the pool and he unwound the towel and dropped it onto a sun lounger. He also looked at her quizzically.

'Obviously apart from having been a boy yourself,' she amended. 'What I mean is, it sounded rather pointed the way you said it.'

He shrugged. 'It was. I had a pretty torrid late-teen period myself. I thought I was invincible when it came to cars, bikes and speed, to girls and the high life.'

Rhiannon stared at him wide-eyed.

He grimaced. 'It's not so unusual, you know.'

'No, I suppose not,' she said slowly. 'I know it's not—especially when you're rich.'

'Oh, absolutely,' he agreed.

'So boxing saved you?'

He nodded. 'Plus a wise mentor. Not that I went on with boxing but I did learn to channel all that energy more productively. I took up polo.'

Rhiannon looked heavenwards. 'How very élite!'

'But competitive, physically challenging and dangerous,' he murmured.

'I'd still like to bet it didn't change your dangerous ways with girls,' she said involuntarily.

'Maybe not,' he conceded and pulled off his T-shirt, 'although this may interest you. They didn't seem to mind.'

She was about to say 'Tell me another!'—but a vision of Lee Richardson as a virile twenty-year-old with all those dark good looks and a bit of a bad-boy reputation planted itself in her mind and she shivered suddenly.

They would and they wouldn't, she thought. Yes, they'd have known they were playing with fire but when he smiled at them as she'd seen him do two days before in an airport lounge, they'd have melted…

They still melted. She herself had melted.

She shook her head to dissolve the image. 'Surely you had plenty of opportunity to channel your energy productively on all those cattle stations in the family?' she objected.

'Of course.' He smiled fleetingly. 'I was mustering cattle as a kid. But I also spent long years at boarding-school then university.'

He stripped off his track pants, revealing a red and white pair of hipster board shorts, and he placed his hands on his hips. 'Why don't you swim too? After a long, hard day slaving over a hot stove you deserve it.'

Rhiannon realised she was staring at him. Again. And again it was hard to stop because he was a work of art. Lean and tall with long, strong legs. Those wide shoulders tapering to a taut, narrow diaphragm; dark, springy hair on his chest and thighs; sleek, smooth, tanned skin sheathing streamlined muscles...

'I—I don't have a costume,' she stammered as she backed away a couple of steps and was brought up short by a pillar.

'You mean you weren't at all tempted to try out our fabulous beaches if nothing else?' he queried gravely but she knew he was laughing at her confusion as he followed her and came to stand right in front of her.

'I was actually going to splash out and buy a new bikini,' she replied as tartly as she was able to, considering that her breathing was ragged and her senses were leaping about like any teenage girl's.

'There's not a lot of difference between some bikinis and a bra and undies,' he said meditatively.

'There is for me,' she contradicted. 'Besides which, with *your* reputation—'

He started to laugh. 'Not only am I reformed and a lot older but I never did make a practice of leaping on girls even in their underwear without an invitation.'

'It's how you go about getting that invitation,' she began but he stopped her short.

'Rhiannon,' he reached out and tucked her hair behind her ear—for once she hadn't done it herself, 'I would say we're both a long way from either the indiscretions or disappointments of our earlier years. So don't blame the effect I have on you,' he looked at her breasts as they moved up and down agitatedly in tune with her uneven breathing, 'on anything but a spontaneous attraction. I will do the same.' His gaze came back to hers and it was curiously sombre and probing.

'I don't trust spontaneous attractions,' she said a little raggedly. 'Not only that—if you must know!— the whole concept irritates the life out of me.' She shook her head frustratedly.

'Because you don't feel you're completely in charge of yourself?' he suggested drily.

Her eyes widened. Had he hit the nail on the head?

'Maybe you should guard against being taken over by your job,' he said then, and smiled lethally. 'A little too much liking for that sense of power it gives you.'

She went to slap his face but he caught her wrist in a hard grip. 'On the other hand,' he said softly, 'you're not kidding me, Rhiannon Fairfax. There's an electric current between us that tells me if you let your guard down your beautiful body would writhe with delight in my bed.'

He looked her up and down and, with sardonic intent, mentally stripped her.

She told herself to breathe evenly in a bid to destroy the images mounting in her mind but it seemed nothing could stop her from visualising herself naked in his arms, drinking in the sleek power of his body, even glorying in his scent of sweat, leather and chalk while he explored her body at whim…

'In the meantime,' he continued after a long, fraught moment as they stared at each other, he coldly and clinically, 'I'm going for a swim. You please yourself but perhaps a cold shower would be a good idea.'

He released her, turned away and dived cleanly into the pool.

* * *

Rhiannon could only come up with one outfit that remotely resembled a party outfit.

'Why didn't I just say no to this?' she asked herself bitterly as she studied her reflection in her bedroom mirror. 'Because he would have cancelled the party, thereby causing considerable chaos or—because I wanted to prove to him he does nothing to me?'

She closed her eyes briefly as she contemplated her disarray beside the pool, and the feeling that she'd like to demolish Lee Richardson one moment, then wake up in his bed the next. Not to mention that insidious little sense that he'd firmly slammed a door in her face again…

She had on a knee-length A-line black skirt that she usually enjoyed wearing but not tonight—other than jeans she had nothing else to cover her legs—and black tights.

She'd teamed it with a coral fine-cotton camisole top with shoestring straps and a drawstring waistline. She wore a four-string fine silver necklace threaded lightly with jade beads and matching long, dangly earrings. Her black shoes had slender heels and were the same ones she'd worn with her grey trouser suit.

She had no evening bag so she tucked a lacy black hanky into her waistband.

She'd washed and dried her hair so it shone and felt bouncy and she'd applied her make-up carefully.

Then there was nothing more to do to herself but she delayed a few minutes longer as she tided her bedroom and bathroom scrupulously. But her conscience got the better of her desire to hold off from any more disturbing encounters with Lee Richardson. The more help she could give Sharon before the party started, the better.

It also struck her that Matt and Mary hadn't arrived yet.

* * *

At a quarter to seven, Rhiannon stepped out onto the east veranda.

The candle glasses were lit, the roses scented the air delicately, all the accoutrements of the meal were in place and the veranda looked lovely.

Lee Richardson was already there, looking impossibly handsome in a grey suit with a black shirt and a silver tie.

She rushed into speech as his gaze flickered down to her legs. 'Aren't they here yet? Do you think they're coming?'

'I—' he broke off and listened '—would say they've just arrived. For someone who had nothing to wear, you've done well, Rhiannon.'

'Thanks,' she mumbled, moving restlessly under his gaze.

He smiled slightly then turned as two people came out onto the veranda.

Matt Richardson didn't resemble his brother much. He was shorter and squarer with curly brown hair, hazel eyes and a wide, engaging smile as he introduced himself to Rhiannon.

'Thank you so much for all this,' he enthused. 'Mary is really grateful, aren't you, sweetheart?' He turned to his wife.

Mary Richardson was stunning. She had red-gold hair, almost turquoise eyes, milky-white skin and a shapely figure that showed no sign of her pregnancy.

She was wearing a low-cut turquoise strapless dress that matched her eyes. It had a frothing ballerina-length skirt, a tight waist and the bodice glittered with sequins. Her high strappy sandals were silver and an exquisite diamond pendant on a platinum chain nestled in the valley between her breasts. She looked sensational.

'Hi!' she said enthusiastically to Rhiannon. 'Wow!' She looked around. 'You have done well! Actually, I've had a great idea,' she said excitedly. 'Why don't you come and work for us permanently, Rhiannon? I'm sure you'd make a great housekeeper!'

Matt flinched and Lee Richardson cast his sister-in-law a speaking look she didn't see because he was standing behind her.

Then another voice said, 'I happen to agree—why don't you give it some thought, Rhiannon?' And Andrea Richardson strolled onto the veranda.

If Mary looked sensational, Andrea topped it. Her hair was piled on top of her head, her strapless, décolleté black gown was moulded to her figure, her skin glowed like ivory and a magnificent ruby necklace matched her lips.

'Thank you,' Rhiannon murmured with a faintly ironic little smile, 'but I have other plans.'

Andrea shrugged and turned away. Her eyes fell on the main table and she tilted her head to one side, then moved forward and repositioned the roses and moved the candelabrum. 'That's better,' she said and turned to glance at Lee with her chin lifted.

Rhiannon took a sharp breath but fortunately Cliff approached at this point. He wore a snowy white shirt, black trousers and a black cummerbund. He had a white napkin over one arm and he carried a small silver tray bearing five frosted glasses of champagne.

'Thanks, Cliff.' Lee took two glasses and handed one to Rhiannon. 'Come and look at the moon,' he added to her.

She hesitated then walked away with him until they were out of earshot of Matt, Mary and Andrea.

The moon was huge and orange as it rested on the dark horizon.

'My apologies,' Lee Richardson said. 'Mary was tactless, so was Andrea.'

Rhiannon flicked her hair back. 'Did you know she was coming, your stepmother?'

'Yes.'

'Well, they probably had no idea they were being tactless—unlike you, earlier. But it doesn't matter.' She took a sip of her champagne.

He looked down at her smooth, fair, bent head. 'Are you talking to me?'

'Only if absolutely necessary.'

He smiled slightly but said, 'Sometimes the truth hurts.' And added before she could take issue with that, 'Why were you crying earlier?'

'Oh, don't start me off again.' She blinked a couple of times and sniffed. 'It was nothing.'

'Thinking of your father?'

Her head came up and she regarded him out of startled brown eyes. 'How did you know?'

He shrugged. 'Not exactly rocket science.'

She sighed. 'Yes, I was. Sometimes it's hard not to feel incredibly sad. But,' she took another sip of champagne and squared her shoulders, 'I'm fully prepared to concentrate on the task to hand tonight. I just hope things don't get out of control. Not that you and your brother couldn't cope but they could be a high-spirited group of people.'

'You can rest easy,' he said. 'I've brought in a security firm.'

Rhiannon's eyes widened. 'Do Matt and Mary know?'

He shook his head. 'Only you and I know and they'll be essentially discreet. Besides which, it's my prerogative. As you mentioned yesterday, there's a lot of very valuable stuff lying around and I would have done it for any group of strangers. The fact that they're Mary's friends is immaterial.'

Rhiannon heaved another sigh but this was a relieved one. She said, however, 'Why didn't I think of that?'

He studied her for a long moment. The coral camisole top showed off more of her delicious curves than he'd seen to-date. The skin of her shoulders was smooth and creamy, her neck was long and slender.

Despite a hard day she looked glossy and perfectly groomed and she smelled nice.

He'd fully expected her to wear trousers or a long skirt, so the shortish skirt—his lips twisted at the thought—was a concession she'd probably been forced, against her better judgement, to make. Her legs, he thought wryly, were enough to tempt any man to think of her in his bed…

'Maybe we make a good team?' he suggested. 'I can fill in the—very few—gaps you leave.'

She half smiled at him then turned her profile away to look at the moon as if suddenly remembering she wasn't talking to him.

He frowned. There'd been an elusive quality in her expression that tantalised him. There were the changes four years had brought to her. Her face had fined down a little and it wasn't as easy to read, but there was still an irrepressible quality to her at times.

There was maturity now, and competence—you

couldn't doubt that—but there was still that hint of vulnerability.

Why the hell should she be turned off men? he wondered suddenly.

Wasn't it something a twenty-two-year-old with a painful experience might lay claim to but a twenty-six-year-old, who had patently got her act together, would be able to put behind her?

He grimaced suddenly. He, of all people, should know how hard some things were to strip from your consciousness; how hard it was not to tar certain situations with the same brush.

He stared down at his champagne glass with narrowed eyes and a hard cast to his mouth. Was he trying to say to himself it was all right for him to decide to leave love alone but another matter for Rhiannon Fairfax?

He started to analyse the thought but the first guests chose that moment to arrive.

Several hours later, the food had been consumed with gratifying enthusiasm and a happy, well-fed throng got down to the dancing end of the evening.

So far so good, Rhiannon thought, and crossed her fingers.

Mary Richardson was in her element; she literally glowed as she mixed with her friends, none of whom had shown any tendency to be wild so far. Some did look way-out, some had raised their eyebrows at the formality of things; they were obviously high-spirited but if that was the worst you could say about them, it was going to be OK.

Both Matt and Lee Richardson had been perfect, Matt in an obviously welcoming, enthusiastic role that seemed to come naturally to him, and he had already met some of the guests, whereas Lee had provided a laid-back yet at the same time subtly commanding presence.

Rhiannon had seen both men and women eye him with unwitting respect, although in the case of some of the women there'd been open speculation that had then transferred to her—Lee had rarely left her side. 'Lucky you' some of those gazes had patently said, causing her to squirm inwardly a little.

And Andrea Richardson, who appeared to have come partnerless to the party, was certainly no wall-flower, but, for those in the know, from the way they ignored each other you could feel the dislike and hostility between Andrea and Lee. You could also see that Mary and Andrea were close.

As the dinner was cleared the DJ, who'd been playing softly in the background, started to wind up to a more throbbing beat.

'You can relax now,' Lee said into her ear as he took her hand.

'I thought I'd been a model of relaxation,' she replied.

'No,' he contradicted. 'You've been a great hostess but anyone who knows you could detect a certain pre-occupation with the food and the service.'

Rhiannon had to laugh. 'Sorry.'

'That's all right but that area of responsibility is at an end now.'

'There's still the coffee and—'

'Rhiannon,' he ordered, 'switch off. Do you dance?'

'Well…' She hesitated.

'Either one does or one doesn't.'

'It's not as simple as that,' she objected. 'One *can* but maybe not that well, for example. One—'

'Forgive me for interrupting but I can't imagine any finishing-school worth its salt sending you out without that skill.'

She stared into his eyes with a tinge of exasperation. 'That's a long time ago. I—'

But this time he put his finger to her lips and drew her into his arms.

They danced well together. Too well together, she came to think as she felt his body against hers, his hand on her waist. It was heady stuff.

She'd have liked to be able to stare over his shoulder but her gaze took to roaming over his thick, short dark hair and she wondered how it would feel to run her fingers through it. Then she found the strong, tanned line of his throat fascinating and, although her hand rested lightly on his shoulder, she could feel the play of his muscles through the stuff of his shirt and the fine silk and mohair of his jacket, and it produced a little thrill of sensation down her body.

That got worse, or more thrilling, as she thought of his lean, hard body only in his swimming shorts as she'd seen it earlier. He'd smelt of sweat then and leather and chalk. Now there was a hint of an astringent cologne and fresh linen, but whichever, she thought with a little trip of surprise she immediately corrected, he was potently attractive to her.

There was still another sensation to deal with. She recalled the mastery of the way he drove his powerful car and the embarrassing comparison it had brought to mind; his mastery over her body in bed.

They definitely weren't in bed but it was his direction, his expert handling of her as they danced that was making her feel as light as gossamer and open to the rhythm of the music. She felt undoubtedly sexy as she moved, not only her feet, but also her body to the beat.

'You didn't honestly believe you weren't any good at this?' he queried as her skirt and her hair belled out and he held her around the waist with both hands.

'I—that wasn't the point I was trying to make,' she replied breathlessly.

'Granted.' He smiled sardonically, pulled her back into his arms and spoke into her ear. 'You were trying to come up with a way to get out of dancing with me. But you're more than a good dancer, Rhiannon.'

'Actually, I'm surprised,' she confessed. 'It's been so long, I *did* think I'd be all thumbs or whatever the equivalent it is with feet. Must be like riding a bicycle.'

'Why has it been so long?'

'All sorts of reasons!' she said lightly.

'No, tell me,' he insisted, and he slowed the tempo deliberately so that they were barely moving and she was pressed against him with his arms wrapped around her back and his hands on her hips.

'You…you can't make me.' She bit her lip as she felt his breath on her neck.

He eyed the flush of exertion in her cheeks and the faint dew of sweat just below her hairline. He noted the slight quiver of her lips and felt the tremors running through her body, the look of surprised uncertainty in her eyes.

He had no need to question the effect on him of her skin and her perfume…

He said, 'I don't need to make you. When two people affect each other the way we do, surely we have to talk about it?'

Rhiannon tried to think straight. The music had moved to another powerful beat but he danced them to the spot where they'd watched the moon rise earlier, where the level of noise was not so high and they could talk more normally.

She stared over his shoulder for a moment. The area they'd left was crowded and the coloured strobe lights the DJ had set up were turning people pink, purple and green.

Mary danced by in the arms of a stranger, no longer turquoise but orange then magenta, still obviously in her element.

Then Andrea drifted past in the arms of a distinguished, silver-haired man, causing her to think briefly about Lee and Andrea. The dislike they felt for each other was almost tangible in the way they so blatantly avoided each other…

She took a deep breath. 'I got really close to a man once. We were engaged and due to get married but it became apparent that I wasn't the heiress he thought I would be so he broke it off. To complicate matters, after he did that I discovered I was pregnant, although I subsequently miscarried.' She paused.

'I wondered about that,' he said quietly.

Her eyes widened. 'How could you possibly…?'

'You spoke about the mood swings pregnancy can bring as if from experience. Two nights ago, in the kitchen,' he added.

'Oh. Yes, I suppose I did.' She looked away. 'Anyway, it turned me right off—no,' she said as he moved, 'I wasn't going to say men; it turned me right off trusting physical attractions, not to mention my own judgement. So—'

'You must have been a lot younger, Rhiannon,' he

broke in. 'I'm not saying it wouldn't have been painful but—'

It was her turn to break in. 'I was twenty-one, and if the level of pain I went through was anything to go by, I'd be mad ever to let it happen to me again.'

He studied the shadows in her eyes but at the same time the imperious tilt of her chin. 'There could have been extenuating circumstances that made it all—all the more catastrophic for you. Your mother, your father.'

'Perhaps,' she conceded, 'but if I ever do marry…'

His lips twisted. 'I'm glad to hear you haven't entirely struck it off your agenda.'

'If I do,' Rhiannon heard herself say, 'it will only be to someone who could never hurt me like that again. Obviously, someone I like and trust, someone who had the potential to build a good life with me, some common ground, but I won't be expecting him to fall madly in love with me and I certainly won't do that either.'

He cupped her shoulders in his hands. 'That sounds like a declaration of independence worthy of a nation let alone a girl.'

'Mr Richardson—Lee,' Rhiannon chose her words with care and she strove to keep her expression neutral, 'I'm not interested in casual affairs and the only reason I'm here is to do a job. N-now,' her voice wobbled slightly for the first time, 'now we've sorted that out, I intend to go back to doing that job. Please excuse me.' And she slipped out of his grasp and away.

CHAPTER FOUR

THE kitchen staff welcomed her back into their bosom enthusiastically with no questions asked other than those concerning the business end of things.

'How did it go? Was it really all right?' Sharon queried.

'It was a triumph,' Rhiannon reassured her. 'It went off wonderfully.' She glanced at her watch, seeing it was past midnight. 'Wow!' she looked around at the gleaming, tidy kitchen. 'You've even done all the dishes!'

'Two dishwashing machines always help! Uh— time to start thinking coffee and bacon-and-egg pies?' Sharon suggested.

'Yes. We'll serve them at one o'clock and hope people take that as the signal to think about going home.'

The bacon-and-egg pie was a secret recipe of Rhiannon's passed down to her from her mother's mother. She'd made a couple of large ones and she'd found they were the perfect way, along with coffee, to wind down a party.

But as she worked alongside Sharon to warm the pies and slice them and make the coffee, her thoughts were elsewhere.

Such as—where had the sudden decision to make a suitable marriage rather than a love match come from?

Well, not exactly a decision but the idea?

Was it the discovery that she was not as immune from a physical attraction as she'd thought?

That doesn't make sense, she told herself. That's exactly what you swore never to be taken in by again.

Then, she contemplated, had Southall got to her? In the sense that it was a home, it had seen years of trust and companionship, growing children—things that were rather like a siren call however much you might mistrust falling in love.

Had it even grown in her, unrealised, from working in other people's homes, with other people's families? Doing, in other words, what she was undoubtedly good at but never for herself...

Maybe, she conceded, but that wasn't going to happen with Lee Richardson, who obviously had his own reasons for remaining "unspoken for".

What were those reasons? she wondered with a sudden frown.

'Rhiannon?'

She blinked and discovered Sharon was staring at her in some puzzlement.

'Sorry. I was thinking about something else. You said?'

'I asked you three times whether we should start serving the coffee.'

'Yes! Would you mind doing it, Sharon? I've had enough of the noise et cetera.'

'Not a problem.' Sharon turned away but turned back. 'Oh. You left your mobile in the kitchen. It rang earlier but by the time I found it, it had switched off. There's probably a message. It's on the counter now.'

'Thanks,' Rhiannon said automatically as she found her mobile then went cold as she brought up the missed call number—her home phone in Sydney.

She always checked in with her aunt twice a day when she was away and had done so today, so there had to be a problem. She pushed some buttons and got her aunt's slightly hysterical message.

Lee found her half an hour later, huddled in a chair in the pool house.

There was no way she could disguise the fact that she'd been crying this time. Her mascara was smudged, her nose was red and she looked wrecked.

He sat down opposite her on the end of a cane lounger. 'Rhiannon? What's happened? Sharon got worried that you'd disappeared after getting a message on your phone.'

'I'm really sorry but I'll have to go home tomorrow,' she said huskily.

'Your father?'

She nodded and shredded a tissue—she'd found a box of them in the pool shower room. 'He's been heading for a hip replacement for some time but he's had a car accident and broken his pelvis as well as damaging some internal organs—it's all become really complicated now, and critical; he needs at least three operations. I've booked myself on the first available flight tomorrow but that's not until ten o'clock.' She choked back a sob.

'Don't.' Lee stood up and pulled her to her feet. 'Come with me.'

'Where? All those people…'

'They've just about all left.' He looked fleetingly grim. 'Anyway, I have a private wing. I'll shout you a brandy.'

Rhiannon was in no condition to argue as the toll of the day on top of her aunt's news started to claim her.

His wing overlooked the east lawn but at the other end of the house from the east veranda.

From what she could see it was a bedroom and living room that had its own entrance from the veranda, and double doors from the living area to the rest of the house.

'No one comes in here except by invitation.' He flicked on a couple of lamps and turned the overhead lights off.

It was a comfortable room in a masculine sort of way. A brown buttoned leather couch and two winged armchairs; a state-of-the art sound and television system in a mahogany cabinet; no flowers, no ornaments but some lovely landscapes on the walls, very outback, Australian ones. And a beautiful, very old ivory chess set on the coffee-table.

'Who do you play with?' she asked with a sniff as he opened a drinks cabinet.

'Cliff,' he said over his shoulder as he reached for two balloon glasses and a bottle of cognac. 'He's a formidable opponent.'

'My father and I—' She stopped and took her bottom lip between her teeth.

'Here.' He handed her a glass and splashed more of the tawny liquid into the second glass. 'Put your feet up,' he suggested.

She hesitated then slipped her shoes off and curled her legs up beside her.

He shrugged out of his jacket and untied his tie. 'So he's safe and sound in hospital for the time being anyway?'

'Yes. But I need to be there!'

'Of course.' Lee sat down in a winged armchair and cradled his glass in his hands. 'I'll drive you down to Coolangatta tomorrow but—'

Before he got time to continue, the house telephone rang.

He answered it but from the monosyllables he uttered it was impossible to tell what was being said at the other end. He put it down and got up.

'I'll be back soon.' He walked over to the sound system and put on a CD and set it to play softly. 'Drink your drink.'

She looked up at him, so tall, so impressive, so—suddenly implacable-looking, and she asked involuntarily, 'Is there a problem?'

'No—nothing to do with you, anyway. Relax, Rhiannon.'

He went out and closed the double doors behind him.

Rhiannon laid her head back as the soft strains of Mendelssohn and *A Midsummer Night's Dream* played through the airwaves, relaxing her even as she wondered, and hoped devoutly not, if the last of the guests hadn't created a fracas or anything of that nature.

She took another sip of her brandy and tried to concentrate on this turn of events but she couldn't think straight and her eyelids grew heavy.

She sipped the last of her brandy to try to keep herself awake but it did the opposite. She fell asleep.

She woke just before dawn.

The red numerals of a digital clock on the bedside table told her this but it struck her slowly that the bedside table in the blue and white guest bedroom at Southall didn't have a digital clock. It had a gorgeous, old-fashioned, miniature carriage clock she'd fallen in love with...

She struggled upright and the next discovery she made was that she was fully clothed apart from her shoes.

She made a strangled little sound and reached out blindly, only to knock a glass of water from the bedside table to the floor with a dull thud.

A lamp went on, illuminating an adjoining room she recognised—Lee Richardson's living room in his private suite, which meant she must be in his bedroom, in his bed!

She sat up with a gasp of horror and Lee himself appeared in the doorway, stretching. He now wore track pants and a sweatshirt.

'Oh, good heavens,' she murmured and flung the bedclothes back preparatory to scrambling out of the bed.

He crossed the floor in a couple of swift strides and sat down on the side of the bed. 'Rhiannon, it's OK. You were out like a light when I came back last night so I thought the simplest thing was to put you to bed here.'

'But...I...what about you?'

He grimaced. 'I slept on the couch.'

She subsided a bit. 'That—that was very kind of you. I'm sorry! I mean, to be such a nuisance. I can't imagine why I would have fallen asleep like that.'

'No?' He raised an eyebrow at her. 'After a day that would have slain most people then some traumatic news?'

She closed her eyes as it all came back to her and

slumped against the pillows with tears beading her lashes.

'Sorry again,' she said thickly and wiped her eyes impatiently with her knuckles. 'I don't usually weep all over the place.'

'I believe you,' he said, and lifted her gently into his arms. 'Look upon me as a shoulder to cry on.'

She didn't cry. She sniffed several times as she rested her cheek on his shoulder and took a couple of shuddering breaths.

Then she quietened and it came to her that she felt a bit like a lone warrior coming in from the cold. Yes, she had her aunt, but otherwise she'd been so alone through the break-up of her father's empire, her mother's death then her own trauma and through the hard-working years that had followed so that some physical comfort, like this, was a taste of heaven.

She felt warmed by it, soothed…she didn't want it to end, she wanted more and the fact that Lee Richardson had been so right about her didn't make the slightest difference…

She raised her head and looked into his eyes. His dark hair was ruffled, and again, she'd been right about designer stubble. It made him look gloriously sexy and desirable and the heavy-lidded way he returned her look added to it.

Her heart started to beat like a muffled drum then she saw him deliberately close his eyes and she felt his arms loosen as if he'd made a sudden decision.

'No,' she breathed and raised her mouth to his, 'don't let me go, I'll fall apart.'

'Rhiannon,' he said against the corner of her mouth, 'with the best will in the world some things can get out of hand.'

'I know but I need you. I need to be reassured I'm…real and that there's *hope* and it isn't all so—so sad. Please.' And she kissed him, the lightest butterfly kiss on his lips.

He groaned and stilled for a moment longer while she held her breath, then he tightened his arms around her and began to kiss her deeply.

She lay back against the pillows and he traced the line of her delicate silver and jade necklace between her breasts, then gently removed her camisole top and black skirt.

She quivered as his fingers strayed to her nipples and he caught his breath as he removed what remained of her clothes. Then he took his hands away and pulled his sweatshirt over his head. He stared down at her for a long moment, her full luscious breasts with their inverted tips starting to flower, the triangle of curls at the top of her thighs, those legs that went on for ever. He drew his hands down the curves of her body, shaping her, sculpting her, before standing swiftly and dispensing with his track pants, turning away briefly as he opened the bedside-table drawer, then joining her naked on the bed.

She sighed with pleasure and went into his arms, and marvelled at the way he made her feel as he cupped her hips. Alive and definitely on the planet, as opposed to how she'd felt earlier but so much more—sexy, desirable and a fitting partner for Lee Richardson.

She gloried in everything that was so fine about him, those powerful shoulders, the hard wall of his chest tapering to a taut waist, his compact hips and long, strong legs.

She drank in the aroma of his smooth, tanned skin…she tasted it.

She played with the sprinkle of dark curls on his chest, she ran her fingers through his hair and etched the blue shadows on his jaw with her fingers.

He caught them and kissed them then took her hand in his down a long, slow exploration of his body that excited her almost unbearably.

She moved into a rhythm against him, she arched her body into his and away. She pressed her breasts against him then away and allowed him to tease and taste her nipples.

She realised dimly at one stage that she'd never before got so carried away in the act of love, she'd never been so giving or so joyfully receptive—and wondered what that made her—but moments later knew that no power on earth could change her reaction.

She was soaring to the dizziest of heights with Lee Richardson and loving it—and she'd been quite right about him. Everything he did to her was masterly and was drawing her towards a fulfilment such as she'd never known.

When it came, it was so strong she had to take the corner of the pillow between her teeth as they shuddered together, sweat-soaked and clinging to each other, their bodies clenching in wonderful sensation…

'All right?' he said what seemed an age later when they'd come down from the heights and he'd drawn the covers over them and was cradling her in his arms.

She could only nod.

He tidied her hair off her face and kissed her lips gently. 'That was—amazing.'

She nodded again then smiled ruefully. 'Sorry.'

He leant his head on his elbow and looked into her eyes. 'What on earth do you mean?'

'I…I just wondered if I…resembled a starving person at a feast.'

'No,' he contradicted and traced the outline of her cheek. 'A wonderful lover and partner.'

She grimaced. 'That's how I'd describe you rather than—'

His fingers moved to her mouth, closing it. 'It was mutual, Rhiannon. We moved each other. We nearly moved both heaven and earth.'

She sighed but it was a contented little sigh, and she rubbed her cheek against his shoulder then she paused, and she lifted her head at the sound of raised voices.

'Who? What?' she asked with concern.

He lay back and rubbed his jaw impatiently. 'The saga continues.'

'What saga?' She looked at him fearfully.

'A friend of one of Mary's friends was caught red-handed nicking a valuable jade figurine. It would have all been glossed over if he hadn't been drunk and made a scene. He claimed he'd only been admiring it, although the security guard saw him put it in his pocket. In fairness, Mary had never met him before but she chose to take his side all the same.

'Things got really difficult after that. She resented the fact that I'd hired security in the first place to check up on her friends. She claimed I'd embarrassed her dreadfully.' He paused. 'But then the crux of the matter really emerged.'

'She doesn't want to be stuck up here at Southall, away from her friends and her old lifestyle?' Rhiannon hazarded.

'Yes. Seeing them again probably consolidated all her woes for her.' He shrugged and played with a strand of Rhiannon's hair.

'I think you're fighting a losing battle, Lee,' Rhiannon said after a moment's silence.

'I think you're right,' he said.

'Is it so important—I mean, is it *so* important for them to live here?' she queried.

He hesitated. 'Not for them, no. Not if it's going to break up their marriage—I *was* hoping to achieve the opposite for Matt.'

'Granted,' Rhiannon agreed then stopped and frowned on the thought that there was so much she didn't know about Lee Richardson. Why, for example, was it important for him to have Southall lived in other than it being more than a bit of a waste for it to lie *unlived*-in?

Then it struck her that all that was of no importance compared to the fact that she was lying in his arms, having just been made love to with exquisite, mind-blowing perfection by him.

She trembled suddenly and he looked down into her eyes alertly. 'Something wrong?'

'N-no,' she stammered. 'Well, this is quite a turn of events, I…I guess, but please believe I don't intend to hold you to it in any way. I mean, I just— I just fell apart a bit but that's not your problem so…' She broke off and closed her eyes as her cheeks grew pink.

'It is quite a turn of events,' she heard him say. 'It's also one that often leads in a certain direction so, for the second time,' he sounded faintly amused, 'will you marry me, Rhiannon?'

She gasped and her lashes flew up. 'You're joking!'

He shook his head and moved the sheet aside so he could play with the silver and jade necklace that lay looped over one breast. 'No.'

'But we've only known each other for a few days!'

'Maybe but we've certainly got to know each other—well.'

'Still…' She attempted to gather her thoughts, not to mention to keep her mind free of what his fingers were doing.

'You could say we've known each other for four years,' he said idly, watching her body not her eyes.

Rhiannon smiled drily. 'You didn't even recognise me. Mind you…' She broke off and grimaced.

'Go on.'

'I almost didn't recognise myself in that awful beret when I got home. I got quite a fright!'

He laughed softly and moved the sheet further aside so he could see her legs. 'I hate to offend you but I would always have recognised these.' He drew his hand down her flank.

She trembled again. 'That's no reason to want to marry me.'

'It's not entirely a bad one. Do you like me?'

'I—I have no reason not to at the moment,' she said disjointedly.

'Trust me?'

'Well, I suppose so—'

'Can you see us having some common ground and being able to build a good life together?'

'Hang on,' Rhiannon murmured as his words resonated through her mind. She sat up and pulled the sheet up. 'That's what I said!'

'I know. All good reasons for us to get married.' He put his arms around her waist and buried his head between her breasts.

She looked down at his thick dark hair and was tempted to run her fingers through it but restrained herself. 'I can't believe I'm having this conversation,' she said dazedly.

He released her and sat up beside her and took her hand. 'Wearing only a necklace and some earrings, and since I'm wearing nothing,' he said gravely, 'not to mention what has preceded this conversation, I think it's particularly appropriate.'

'No.' Her hand shook in his. 'No. Something's going on that I don't understand.' She turned to him suddenly. 'Has it to do with Southall?'

'Why do you ask?'

'Just a hunch—but a strong one. Don't forget,' she added, suddenly remembering herself, 'you were the one who told me you were turned off "being spoken for", possibly for the duration.'

'Rhiannon,' he said deliberately and took her chin in his fingers, 'the most significant thing that's happened is that we came together almost as if we were made for each other.'

'But,' her lips quivered, 'if I hadn't been so distressed it wouldn't have happened.'

'Don't kid yourself,' he advised. 'We wondered about each other four years ago. We started to wonder almost as soon as we came into contact again.'

She blushed.

'And that tells its own tale,' he said thoughtfully with his blue gaze scanning the tide of colour in her cheeks, and he put his arm around her and kissed the top of her head.

'All the same,' she said against his shoulder, 'I need to know where I stand. I mean…' She bit her lip frustratedly.

The house phone in his living room rang.

He swore beneath his breath. 'Matt, no doubt. Stay here, I'll deal with it.'

But as he got out of bed and pulled on his tracks and sweatshirt, Rhiannon came to life and started to get out of bed too. 'I need a shower and I need to get going! Oh, I can't believe this, I haven't had time to think of my father except just before we—we—'

'Made earth-shattering love?' His eyes glinted briefly then he sobered. 'Never mind, we'll think of your father together. We've also got plenty of time to make that flight. Have your shower here. The bathroom's through there. You can borrow my robe. I won't be long and we'll get going as soon as we've sorted a couple of things out.'

'But Lee,' she said urgently with a kind of bemused panic in her eyes.

'Rhiannon,' he drew her slim naked body into his arms, 'please don't go away. You're right, we need to talk.' He looked into her eyes and his were deadly serious.

She showered and washed her hair in a curiously feverish way as her thoughts alternated between her father and Lee.

Then she folded herself into his navy-blue robe and padded through to the living room.

Lee came in from the house almost immediately, bearing a tray.

'Tea and toast, the limit of my capabilities.' He put it down on the coffee-table and walked over to her. 'How does that feel?' He took in her damp, combed hair and clean, shiny face. 'Did I do any damage?'

He flicked the robe open.

'No! I mean, I—I didn't look,' she stammered and attempted to close the robe.

He resisted her easily and took a long, comprehensive look down her body. 'You know, you are definitely a ten,' he said softly, and closed the robe, apparently satisfied.

'What…what's going on out there?' she asked in some confusion.

He smiled at her agitation and led her to the settee. 'Have a seat, I'll pour the tea. Matt caved in last night, not without Andrea's help, and he and Mary are moving back to the Brisbane apartment we have today.'

'You shouldn't—' Rhiannon bit her lip but decided to soldier on '—you shouldn't be judgemental. It's their life and only they can sort it out.' She paused then looked at him alertly. 'So you won't need me any more?'

'Yes, I will.' He returned her look in a way that brought her out in goose pimples.

'I mean on a professional basis,' she said with an effort.

'No, and never again,' he agreed, 'but a personal basis is another matter.'

'Lee…' She stopped as he put a cup and saucer in front of her and offered her a slice of Vegemite toast—the Vegemite would have amused her in other circumstances.

'Rhiannon,' he sat back with his cup and saucer, 'yes, I did have reason to believe I wouldn't take to marriage too well. Like you, I found that love wasn't all it was cracked up to be, it was a rather bitter experience and it made me,' he shrugged, 'quite cynical. So you could say we're two of a kind.' He looked at her penetratingly.

She could only stare back wide-eyed.

'And yes, you're right,' he went on, 'Southall has a part to play in things although,' his lips twisted as he glanced through to the bedroom, 'what you termed as "this turn of events" is far the more crucial.' He paused.

'What part *does* Southall play?' she asked huskily.

He fiddled with his teaspoon and she watched him, the way his dark hair fell in his eyes, his frown of concentration.

He said, at length, 'It goes back to my father. Andrea, as you've no doubt seen for yourself, was half his age when she conned him into marrying her and she made him give up his Australian life and take her to the south of France to live.' This time as he paused he looked faintly quizzical. 'Now, I know you'll probably think that's their affair and you'd be right.'

He sipped his tea and looked into the distance and his expression changed drastically to one so grim and cold, Rhiannon actually shivered. 'That she should want to come back now and make Southall her head-quarters—the home that my mother created and loved and where she died—is my affair and I don't intend to allow it to happen.'

'But—' Rhiannon frowned '—how…I still don't understand.'

He paused, then he said, 'Southall was left to me and Matt but a clause was added to my father's will and I have no doubt Andrea was responsible for it. It states that if, after his death, neither Matt nor I are living here *with our spouse or family*, Andrea should have the right to make it her home for as long as that situation continues.'

Rhiannon pushed her fingers through her hair. 'So…?' She stopped as things tumbled into place in her mind rather like fruit on a gaming machine. 'So that's why you wanted Matt and Mary to—to be in residence so she couldn't move in?' she breathed. 'That's why you hired me to help make it work and— But that's so manipulative and…' She couldn't go on.

'Manipulative?' He smiled drily. 'Not entirely—it was also what Matt wanted. As to who is more manipulative, my stepmother or myself, that's debatable.'

'What do you mean?' she whispered.

'When Matt married Mary and announced they'd live here, Andrea obviously gave up any idea of being able to put that clause to work for her. But Matt took Mary to meet Andrea in France on their honeymoon— he wanted to show her our father's grave—and Andrea, I guess, sensed that Mary would find it difficult to adjust to this lifestyle, and to that end she's been working on Mary ever since.'

Rhiannon drew a long, shaky breath. 'I—see.'

'Do you? I wonder,' he said.

Rhiannon tried to collect her thoughts. 'Look,' she gestured, 'I guess this is an outsider's view but, for what it's worth, she is astonishingly beautiful and your father may have been lost and lonely without your mother, maybe experiencing a mid-life crisis?' she suggested.

He grimaced. 'You're very forgiving but, yes, probably all of those things. To go overboard like that, however…'

He shrugged.

'Maybe,' she said slowly, 'that clause was not only her influence but *his* way of trying to ensure some *place* for her in the family if he died? Maybe that's what she feels she needs, a place somewhere now she's alone?'

'At the moment, all she's succeeded in doing is tearing us apart,' he said cynically. 'Matt feels he's letting me down by going, but he would be letting

Mary down if he stayed. Then there's the possibility that once Andrea digs in it could take a court case to get her out whenever I marry.'

She stared at him. 'So…?' Her lips parted, her eyes changed from stunned to accusing. 'That's where I come in? Now you can't have Matt and Mary to keep her out you want me to— Oh, no!' She put her toast down untasted and stood up, poised for flight.

But he was too fast for her as he got rid of his tea, stood up and he took her wrist. 'Is it as bad as it sounds? How do you feel about Southall, Rhiannon?'

'I, well, I love it but all the same—'

'And my mother would have approved of you entirely. She *was* very much like you in the way she got out and did things. She would have adored the way you love this place and all the things in it.'

Rhiannon rubbed her face with her free hand. 'You're leading me into all sorts of traps again,' she cried.

'Yes, but I wasn't the one who brought them up in the first place. I also love Southall but I haven't enjoyed rattling around in it on my own, so we'd have that common ground you mentioned.'

'Why did I ever open my mouth?' she asked despairingly.

A lightening grin creased his face and the glint in his eyes was perfectly wicked. 'You have a habit of bringing up pertinent points,' he reminded her. 'Like your legs.'

She closed her eyes in deep frustration.

'There's more,' he said. 'I could ensure your father gets the best care available. Somewhere close to here so you'd be able to spend plenty of time with him. And if he and your aunt would like to live with us, she'd be welcome. There's a free cottage in the grounds and it's rather attractive.'

Rhiannon's eyes flew open then she went quite still.

'You…you would do all that? Just to keep your stepmother out of Southall?'

He shook his head. 'No, because I want to. I do have another option regarding Southall. I could sell it, thereby taking it out of the equation for ever.'

She made a protesting little sound in her throat then her eyes dilated at how much of a give-away it would have been.

'My sentiments entirely,' he echoed.

Rhiannon trembled. 'I—I still don't know what to say.'

'Sit down and drink your tea,' he suggested.

She looked in two minds then slowly sat down again and drank her tea and ate half her toast before she said with decision, 'I can't do it, Lee. I really appreciate your…your thoughtfulness towards my father but what I have to offer in return is minimal, so I would always feel beholden to you and—and I don't think I'd be very good at that.'

'We'll deal with the minimal aspect later—although preserving my home from a woman *on* the make is not minimal, I can assure you,' he returned swiftly. 'But would I be right in thinking this situation with your father is not only much graver now but has come before you're financially prepared for it?'

Rhiannon swallowed. 'A bit,' she conceded. 'I won't be able to afford private care for him but—but maybe I could get a loan. I—'

'I could have offered you a loan but—'

'Oh no—'

'Don't say a word,' he commanded. 'But I'd much

rather be married to you because what you have to offer in return is not minimal at all. We'd be good together, Rhiannon. In bed and out of it. I have cattle stations to show you, a whole new world for you, and one I'm—' he paused '—I'm tired of running on my own.'

She stared at him wide-eyed. 'I have no idea—I mean, I know I told you I enjoyed them but I would have no idea how to run cattle stations!'

'I wouldn't expect you to run them *per se* but to have an energetic, capable companion who is also gorgeous and prepared to be involved would be great. Incidentally,' he eyed her from head to toe, 'you didn't expect to sleep with me like that then simply walk away, did you?'

'I...' Colour flooded her cheeks. 'I didn't set out to sleep with you, so—'

'You did such a great job of it, I can't wait to experience you when you really set your mind to it!'

Rhiannon bit her lip this time and trembled visibly.

He half smiled and put his arm around her. 'I loved every minute of it.'

'But we are—we are virtually strangers,' she mumbled.

'If you can come up with another stranger who makes you feel the way I do, I'll retire gracefully,' he said gravely and started to open her robe again.

Rhiannon took a despairing breath as his hands slid over her breasts but it didn't stay despairing for long. It became ragged as he set off tremors of desire deep within her; lovely sensations that washed through her right to her toes as well as activating that warm, secure feeling of having come in from the cold.

It dawned on her that she might be fighting a losing

battle, much as one small part of her mind was sending out danger signals…

But, if nothing else, to have the burden of her father's health taken care of so he could get the very best of treatment would be such a relief, could she afford to spurn it?

CHAPTER FIVE

A MONTH later, Rhiannon woke up to her wedding day.

It had been a whirlwind few weeks, Lee had worked fast.

Her father had been relocated to a private hospital on the Gold Coast by air ambulance and had his hip replacement as well as operations for his broken pelvis and damaged organs. He'd been heavily sedated before the operations so had had little idea of what was going on. It had been touch and go a couple of times but the expert advice now was that he'd make a full recovery.

An apartment had been rented close to the hospital so Rhiannon didn't have the daily drive to and from Southall, and she shared it with her aunt.

What with all the coming and going between Sydney—she and her aunt had packed up their rented house—the long hours spent in the hospital with her father while he drifted in and out of consciousness between operations, Lee had made no demands on her.

In fact they hadn't shared a bed again, although, when they'd been together, the closeness that had sprung up between them after that spectacular 'turn of events' had been tangible.

She was still amazed by it. He seemed to be able to

read her mind and judge her moods accurately. It was almost as if they'd known each other for a long time.

It was only when she wasn't with him that some doubts crept in. Did she read him as well as he read her, for example? Or was there a core to Lee Richardson that remained a mystery to her? That was a particularly persistent little doubt she found hard to shake.

Another one was the memory of the times he'd, speaking figuratively, shut a door in her face. For some reason she couldn't seem to forget them...

Her other concern remained that, whatever he might like to think, what he was doing for her was little short of monumental in terms of the peace of mind it was going to bring her.

She'd also been tempted to present her father with a *fait accompli* regarding her marriage but Lee had flatly disagreed. Her objections had been that her father would worry she'd married a rich man for his sake and would hate not only that but also being beholden to a man who was one of his creditors.

Lee had said simply, 'We'll just have to convince him otherwise, then. And unless you're in the know, there's no way to connect me with the trucking company.'

'But I don't want him to have anything to worry about at the moment!' she'd said. 'That's why if it's done, at least—at least he can't upset himself trying to change things.'

'No, I don't agree.' Lee had said it quietly but definitely.

She blinked. 'I feel as if I'm being held to ransom,' she'd said slowly.

'You are,' he'd agreed. 'Look, either we're going to

do this and do it openly, or not. In other words, either we agree we have good grounds for this marriage apart from your father or we don't do it. And if we do agree on that, we have no reason to hide it.'

She looked away. 'It's not that.'

'Good.' He studied her keenly, the blue shadows beneath her eyes brought on by the strain of everything she'd gone through. 'So you do agree with me?' He reached out and traced the line of her cheek with his fingertip.

She trembled.

'Rhiannon?'

She looked back at him. 'All right. Let's,' she swallowed, 'do it today.'

'That's my girl,' he said quietly, and proceeded to bowl her father right over when they visited him in hospital that day so that when he left Rhiannon and Luke Fairfax alone, her father seemed to be genuinely happy for her.

'My dear, oh my dear,' his face lit up as he studied her, although he was in traction and still experiencing discomfort and pain, 'I've been so worried for so long that you'd put off any romantic episodes on my account! But why—I must say I like him very much— but why haven't I heard anything about him?'

'I wanted to be very sure first, Dad. I—actually met him a few years ago but, well, I am sure now. We,' she lowered her lashes and knitted her fingers together, 'do good things for each other.'

When she looked up, her father was watching her intently. But all he said was, 'So that's why I got spirited up to Queensland?'

'Yes, Dad,' she said steadily, and told him about Southall.

'But—'

'No buts,' she said gently. 'I need you close to me and Di is happy to come too.'

Later, Rhiannon couldn't help wondering if her father would, when he was in better shape, start to wonder about the financial side of things, but all she could offer herself was the thought that the deed would be done then...

Her aunt Diana had accepted the move to Southall gratefully so she could be close to her brother, although not without grave reservations at first. In fact Diana had wormed, or rather divined, some of the truth out of her niece.

'Are we talking a *coup de foudre* here?' she demanded to know. 'What else could explain it coming so—so out of the blue?'

'No! No,' Rhiannon amended less forcefully. 'But we just—click. And because he's able to and wants to help Dad we decided not to muck around.'

Diana Fairfax was tall and middle-aged, often vague, often had paint spattered hands—she dabbled in oil paintings as well as music—but at other times she was astonishingly acute. 'Rhiannon, I know how much you care for your father but isn't that a little extreme?'

'It's not only for Dad. We have an awful lot in common. We do...' Here, Rhiannon paused then went on a little hurriedly, 'We do feel quite strongly about each other.'

Diana blinked. She also had sherry-brown eyes. 'Maybe, but shouldn't you take a bit longer to get to know each other?'

Rhiannon simply shook her head.

'I see.' Diana stared at her niece. 'I gather your mind is made up, Rhiannon.'

Rhiannon nodded.

'So nothing I say or do is going to change it?'

Rhiannon shook her head again.

'Do you know, I've seen that stubborn look in your eyes since you were about two years old?'

'Me? Stubborn?'

'Yes, you,' Diana replied. 'In fact it would be fair to say there were times when you were a right handful and not only as a child!'

'I was not!' Rhiannon looked injured then a little shamefaced. 'Maybe sometimes, but Di, I am going to do this.'

'Hmm… Well, I'll just say this. If ever you need a confidante, I'm here. When do I get to meet him and are you absolutely sure he wants me too?'

'Quite sure. Oh, Di, you're going to love it up there. There's a local operatic society. According to Sharon—she's the housekeeper—there's a real opening for a piano teacher and it's just so beautiful. And you'll meet him tomorrow.'

You couldn't exactly say that Lee Richardson had bowled Diana over but he must have made a good impression because her aunt had seemed to relax a bit on the subject of her niece's unexpected marriage.

Telling Matt and Mary had also involved some subterfuge. Lee and Rhiannon had driven down to the Brisbane apartment to break the news…

'What?' Matt Richardson said incredulously. 'But you barely know each other!'

'We actually met four years ago,' Lee replied.

Mary Richardson, who'd obviously got over the trauma of the party, took another tack. 'How exciting! There, you see, darling,' she turned to Matt, 'I told you things would work themselves out with Southall! Although Andrea might not be best pleased…but I did wonder what she'd do with herself up there, anyway.'

'All the same…' Matt Richardson shot his wife an exasperated glance then eyed his brother concernedly.

But Lee took Rhiannon's hand. 'It would be fair to say we can't actually wait,' he murmured and looked at Rhiannon for corroboration.

Her reaction couldn't have been better if she'd rehearsed it. She had gone pink beneath those dark blue eyes and the little glint in them. Pink and flustered; trapped by the sensual memories of their lovemaking in a way that told its own tale.

Not, she thought as she lay in bed in the cottage her aunt and father would occupy on the Southall estate on the morning of her wedding, that she could have rehearsed that blushing, flustered air she'd given off. It was something that only came naturally—it had certainly reassured Matt Richardson.

Nor had she been perfectly honest with her aunt by omission. She'd left out the fact that she and Lee set each other alight physically, but had Diana seen that for herself?

As for how Andrea Richardson had got the news, and taken it, she had no idea. She hadn't asked and Lee hadn't volunteered anything.

What really exercised her mind as she lay in bed that morning was how *she* felt, though.

She had butterflies in her stomach and she was possessed of a sense of unreality. Yes, she liked Lee more and more and she *was* physically set alight by him, but there was something she couldn't quite put her finger on, something holding her back. Not that she could get out of it now...

She sat up feeling suddenly panic-stricken and had to take some deep breaths.

What had she done? Why hadn't this panic gripped her before, long before her wedding morning? Yes, she'd always had some reservations but what was the real core of her fear now?

It hit her suddenly and she couldn't believe she hadn't thought of it before but she had had an awful lot on her mind—what had been so damaging about his previous love life that had turned Lee Richardson off any commitment to a woman until she'd fallen apart in his bed?

It had to have been something really significant he couldn't put behind him until she slept with him as if he were the last man on the planet!

It had to account for the times when she felt as if she was running into a brick wall—such as his immovability on her wish to get married first and tell her father later. Come to that, his immovability on any terms but his own—which included the whole concept of this marriage.

Why didn't I ask? she marvelled. Because I was under too much pressure to think straight? Because, secretly, I was afraid of what I would hear?

But what difference would it have made, whatever I heard? We've both acknowledged love didn't work for us so this was the only way to go...

Yet she couldn't shake the curious feeling of something hovering on the edge of her mind, some mysterious key, something she should be able to work out but couldn't...

She gave up with a frustrated shake of her head and concentrated on the fact that, even if you were sworn off falling in love, you were always vulnerable to a man who set you alight physically. It was the nature of things.

So how was she going to retain her independence and keep her side of the bargain at the same time?

Take a leaf out of his book? she wondered. Maintain an elusive certain something he couldn't reach?

That's it, she thought, and breathed a sigh of relief. There's a core of me I won't allow any man to reach or break again. She lay back feeling somewhat reassured.

The wedding ceremony was performed next to the rose garden.

It was a clear, sunny day and the service, carried out by a marriage celebrant, commenced at noon.

Curiously, considering what she'd done for a living, Rhiannon had had little input, but someone had, she divined.

There were beautiful cloths over the small table in the garden and the bigger one on the east veranda. There were roses in vases and she carried a bouquet of the palest pink ones.

It was a small gathering. Matt and Mary Richardson, Diana, Christy and her father, Sharon and a middle-aged couple she'd never met but was later introduced to as Lee's PA and his wife, George and Judy Benson. She also learnt later that they'd organised the wedding.

It was a simple ceremony and she wore an ivory silk outfit her aunt had helped her to choose. It had a short skirt and loose jacket but the austerity of it was relieved by beautiful intricate pearl beading on the jacket. A silver comb that duplicated the pearl beading held back her hair.

Unfortunately, the butterflies in her stomach came back to plague her as soon as she saw Lee.

He wore a dark suit with a cream shirt and a cream rosebud in his lapel. He looked devastatingly attractive but—a stranger!

Then he turned and saw her, and a smile grew in his eyes as he took her in, especially her legs, and he did the only thing that was going to propel her forward rather than taking flight. He held out his hand to her.

'Big day.'

Rhiannon turned away from the view. They were in the honeymoon suite of a beautiful resort on the Bloomfield River in far North Queensland.

They'd driven down to the coast with her aunt, still dressed for their wedding, and shared a bottle of champagne with her father. Then they'd changed and flown to Cairns and on to the Bloomfield, where they'd been ferried from the landing strip across the river by boat.

The resort nestled in an exotic mountainous rain-forest area but beyond the wide mouth of the river another, equally splendid, scenario beckoned—the tropical waters of the Coral Sea and the Great Barrier Reef.

The suite, a bungalow on stilts called a bure, was exquisitely furnished in cool creams and whites against the dark background of native timbers and a soaring ceiling. The huge double bed had a billowing mosquito net caught up decoratively on the wall behind it.

She turned from the veranda railing to Lee who was lounging against the door frame. 'Yes, but this is something else.'

'I hoped you'd like it.'

'How long will we stay?' she queried as she made the discovery that she was feeling all jittery again. She knew nothing about the most important thing to do with this man, the thing that had turned him off commitment until she'd appeared on the scene and proved to be so suitable, not only for his lifestyle but also as a weapon against his stepmother's aspirations.

He shrugged. 'As long as you want to.' He held out his hand to her.

She stared at it then lifted her eyes to his. 'I feel— I feel a bit strange,' she said huskily.

He now wore khaki trousers and a blue and white checked shirt, she wore jeans and a white blouse.

He raised an eyebrow and took back his hand. 'How so?'

'It's a bit like a dream. It's,' she hesitated, 'it's hard to believe we're married.'

He glanced at her rings, a gold band and a beautifully cut baguette emerald with two diamonds beside it. 'It did happen.'

'Yes, I know.' She pushed back her hair and tried to concentrate. Then she smiled, a fleeting, wry little smile. 'I think I know how every wife who's had her husband chosen for her—may not even have met him!—felt and feels.'

'That's,' he gestured, 'a bit far-fetched in our case, don't you think?'

She spread her hands. 'It's almost as if it happened in another life. I'm sorry, I feel quite a wimp! I don't—' she shook her head '—well, I don't know exactly *how* I feel.'

He smiled slightly. 'There's a beautiful pool here. We have an hour or so before dinner. Like to try it?'

Rhiannon blinked at him but, rather than contesting this apparent *non sequitur*, she grabbed it with both hands, speaking figuratively. 'Definitely! Well, it's warm enough and I do now have a new bikini—uh…' She paused, looking more confused than ever.

'Go to it, Mrs Richardson,' he said. 'I'll grab my things and meet you there.'

After he'd changed swiftly and left her alone, Rhiannon sank onto the bed with her bikini in her hands and her cheeks hot.

Why was she acting like a terrified virgin? she wondered. Not that it was that so much; it was more that she felt as if she were standing at an open doorway looking on to a blank view.

She clicked her tongue exasperatedly and started to shed her clothes.

The bikini was emerald and white, quite accidentally matching the colours of her engagement ring. She put it on and wrapped a gauzy, silvery sarong round her, knotting it between her breasts. She slid her feet into flat silver sandals and drew a deep breath.

The path to the pool led over a suspension bridge that spanned a small ravine with water flowing down it. She paused for a moment to look at the ferns and lush foliage then continued her journey towards the unknown…

Stop it, she commanded herself. You're being ridiculous!

There was no one in sight at the pool area and only Lee in the pool, lapping it in a strong, even crawl.

She shed her sarong and dived in. The water was warm and silky and she came up and spread her arms luxuriously.

A pair of strong arms slid round her waist from behind and a deep, husky voice said into her ear, 'I don't believe we've met.'

'We…haven't?' she replied after a startled moment.

'No.' He trod water and she didn't have to do anything but lie back against him.

'But—' she began.

'Shhh…' her captor said. 'I'm actually a dangerous pirate in disguise with a taste for untraditional sirens, two-legged ones. I'm renowned for capturing them—the longer their legs the better—and taking them away to a distant dark shore, where, by the light of a bonfire, I have my ravishingly seductive way with them before discarding them.'

Rhiannon made a strange little sound in her throat.

'At least,' he paused and cupped her breasts, 'that's how my wife seems to look upon me. As if, at the very least, I've caused an ocean of tears to be shed over me. You might even say she's viewing me with deep suspicion.'

Rhiannon bit her lip. 'Lee…'

Once again his hands moved on her slippery body and she trembled as his fingers slid beneath the elastic of her bikini bottom to cradle her hip. Then he floated backwards, taking her with him until they could stand.

He turned her round in his arms so she was facing him.

Both their heads were sleek and wet, they had droplets on their eyelashes. His upper body was smooth, muscled and tanned whilst hers was curvy and creamy pale.

'Rhiannon,' he paused at the same time as he traced the valley between her breasts, 'we made a commitment, one that I fully intend to keep.'

She stared deeply into his eyes for a long moment and saw that he meant it. Then she sighed a quivering little sigh and said, 'Would you do me a favour?'

'Yes.'

'Would you kiss me? I seem to need it rather badly.'

'By all means.' He lowered his mouth to hers.

When they finally drew apart, and she got her breath back, she was struck by a sudden thought. 'Are we the only two people on the planet?'

'No. There are other people staying here but I'm reliably informed they've gone to Cooktown on a day trip—ah,' he added, 'from the sounds I hear, they may be returning.'

'Would it be a good idea to remove ourselves to a more private place?'

He laughed down into her eyes. 'You're full of good ideas, Rhiannon—yes, it would!'

They were laughing as they scrambled out of the pool and fled down the path towards their bure.

They were still laughing and cool and damp but the laughter died as hunger took its place, not for food but each other.

'It's been a long four weeks,' he murmured as he unclipped her bikini top.

'Thank you for waiting.'

'I can't exactly say my pleasure,' he looked amused, 'but sometimes it's important to get the timing right.' He drew the top off slowly and dropped it to the floor. 'Now these,' he gently stroked her breasts, 'believe it or not, have almost taken precedence over your legs in my imagination.'

She gasped as he pressed her nipples between his fingers.

'And I have a very fertile imagination when it comes

to you, Rhiannon,' he added, studying her through half-closed lids.

'You do?'

'Mmm… Often at all the wrong moments too. How about you?' His hands slid down to her hips, pushing her bikini bottom down.

She said unevenly, 'I have been known to experience a curious ambivalence towards you.' She wriggled and stepped out of her bikini bottoms. 'One moment I've felt like demolishing you, the next, wishing I was waking up in your bed.'

'That's been quite apparent,' he said gravely. 'I don't know how I survived your demolition moments.'

She chuckled. 'They were actually quite feeble, as you very well know.'

He drew her into his arms and said into her hair, 'You're welcome to demolish me right now, as powerfully as you like.'

'I have a better idea,' she said softly. 'I know we don't have a deserted shore or a bonfire but we could turn on a lamp and you could demonstrate your ravishing seduction technique. I mean to say, I didn't give you a lot of time to—well, you know what I mean, last time around.'

He raised his head and looked into her eyes. 'You sure you're not laughing at me?'

'Perish the thought.'

'Very well. Stay right there. I'll be back in a moment.'

She stayed whilst he moved into the lounge and presently came back with two glasses of champagne. He handed her one and waited while she sipped it, then he tipped some of his over her breasts.

She gasped and gasped again as her nipples

exploded with the shock of it and he bent his head and tasted each one in turn. Then he got rid of their glasses and picked her up to lay her on the bed.

'Turn over,' he commanded and she rolled onto her stomach obediently with her arms stretched above her head.

He lay down beside her with his head propped on one hand and swept the other down her back in languorous strokes, pausing at the downy hollows above her hips before sculpting the curves of her bottom and tracking through the creases at the tops of her thighs.

'Oh,' she breathed as a fire started to build in the pit of her stomach and she moved luxuriously, 'don't stop, that's divine.'

And she parted her legs with a husky little sound that was a mixture of desire and an invitation.

His fingers slipped between her thighs and she felt herself grow warm and wet as the fire in her belly grew.

'Am I allowed to have any say in this ravishment, because if not it might be too late before—?'

'Be my guest. If there's one thing I believe in equality about it's this.'

She turned over and sat up. 'Lie still, then. Don't move a muscle.' And she eased herself on top of him, having assured herself he was as ready as she was. 'There.' She smiled secretively as her body accepted his erection. 'How about that?'

'Am I allowed to talk?'

'No.' She put her fingers to his lips then ran them through his hair and lifted herself so her nipples were just brushing the hard wall of his chest.

He took a tortured breath and claimed her with ever more powerful thrusts and she received them with mounting excitement then an explosion of sensation...

* * *

'That was even closer than the last time,' he said, when they came down from the heights. 'How did I do?'

Rhiannon moved cautiously then laid her cheek on his chest with a sigh of contentment. 'What you don't know is that I'm Secretary-General of the Siren's Union, the two-legged division, that is, come to check you out. Not only you but your workplace relations et cetera, et cetera.'

'Now, that was sneaky,' he said. 'You might have let me know.'

'You…well, I'll have to think out my report, but I can reassure you I won't be placing any bans on you at the moment.'

He grinned wickedly then sobered and tilted her chin so he could look into her eyes. 'No. Really. Are you happy to be married to me now, Rhiannon?'

'Yes,' she said simply then looked concerned. 'I don't know why I was so—'

'I do,' he interrupted. 'It was a leap into the unknown. You were under enormous pressure but we can make this work. By the way, I've got something for you.' He reached over and pulled open the bedside-table drawer. He took out a long, slim black leather box tooled with gold and handed it to her.

Rhiannon took a breath and pressed the catch with her mind reeling because she'd seen one such box before, on her eighteenth birthday…

It was an exquisite string of Australian South Sea pearls, some of the most sought-after cultured pearls in the world.

She exhaled slowly and lifted the string from its bed of velvet. She knew a bit about pearls and could tell that their lustre, the beauty of light being reflected from the surface of the pearl, was exceptional, so was the white-pink colour and she could feel the perfect synergy—the way the strand draped like a piece of silk. The clasp was eighteen-carat gold, pave-set with white diamonds.

'Oh, Lee,' she said huskily, 'you shouldn't have. I don't know what to say.'

'You don't have to say anything.' He took the strand from her and put it on her. 'As soon as I saw them I knew I wouldn't rest until I gave them their perfect setting. Yes,' he trailed the strand with his fingers—it came to rest between her breasts, 'I was right.'

'Does that mean...?' She looked at him wide-eyed.

He smiled into her eyes. 'It means you may wear them at other times, for example when you're dressed, at your peril.'

Her lips curved. 'If that means what I think it means I might be safer just wearing them in bed.'

'Depends what you mean by "safer".'

She pushed her fingers through his hair. 'Well, better prepared, then. Thank you so much.'

'On this occasion,' he took her in his arms and lay back with her, 'I can say my pleasure, ma'am.'

Four days later they left the Bloomfield.

Days when they swam, or beach-combed, they fished, but above all they got to know each other better.

Of course, Rhiannon reasoned, while their passion for each other was so white-hot there was not a lot they were going to dislike about each other.

Nor could she ever forget how he'd helped her over the barrier of nerves and whether she'd done the right thing she'd been unable to break through on their wedding day but they did seem to have a lot in common.

Little things. They were both action people, they

had the same taste in music, they were cryptic-cross-word fans and had some hilarious times doing them together, including a strip form of the game that was new to Rhiannon and led on to other things...

But all the same, she had moments of—perhaps disbelief was the best way to put it, she thought, and one of them created some tension between them.

She was watching a travel programme on television one evening, in the bedroom, while Lee was talking to George Benson, his PA, on the phone in the lounge.

She was changed and in bed when the programme touched on the French Riviera, and it brought Andrea to mind for Rhiannon in a curious way.

She suddenly remembered Mary's remark about what Andrea would do with herself up at Southall, anyway, and it seemed to make sense—what would Andrea have done with herself at Southall? Yes, a wonderful home but far removed from the trendiness and glamour of the Riviera for someone who was heavily into fashion. So why would she want to make it her headquarters?

And why did it activate a deep sense of unease in her she couldn't explain? Rhiannon wondered. The connection with Southall? That led to the disturbing thought, a thought that grew less comfortable by the day, that she didn't know if, without that clause in his father's will, Lee would have married her.

But that didn't make sense when their honeymoon, at least, was going so well. Or, she thought with a sense of dread now, was it going too well for her? To the extent that she hated the thought that Lee had had every valid reason for marrying her except the one that mattered most—he hadn't fallen in love with her...

'Penny for 'em?'

She looked up at Lee with a frown. 'I— No, nothing.'

'There's ways and means of getting it out of you, lady,' he drawled, and joined her on the bed.

'Lee,' she sat up and hugged her knees, 'what's on the agenda for tomorrow?'

It was his turn to frown. 'Is that a kind of "I have a headache" *non sequitur*?'

'Funnily enough,' she said slowly, 'my head doesn't feel too good at the moment.'

He sat up and stared into her eyes for a long moment. 'OK,' he got off the bed, 'I'll get you an aspirin and sleep on the couch.'

'Oh, I didn't mean—'

He shrugged and interrupted her. 'I've got some more calls to make anyway and the couch makes up as a bed.' He turned away and went through to the bathroom.

Rhiannon stared after him and knew she'd had another door shut in her face. She spent a miserable, uneasy night on her own. Had she asked for it?

In light of her proclamation of independence—how foolish had that been? she asked herself—was she entitled to be disturbed because keeping Andrea out of Southall had been a big part of Lee's motivation?

And what was hovering on the edge of her mind but refusing to reveal itself?

The next morning, she woke late to find him sitting on the side of the bed with a cup of tea for her.

She stretched, yawned then she remembered and her eyes flew to his face.

'Feeling better?' he queried as he set the cup and saucer on the bedside table.

'I— Yes.' She bit her lip.

He surveyed her discomfort. 'It's OK,' he said quietly. 'I suspect I was a bit of a bastard last night. As you once remarked to me, men can have very fragile egos.'

Her eyes softened and she put her hand into his. 'Not only men.'

'Well,' he closed his fingers around hers, 'we're off to the Hope Isles today, it looks to be a magnificent day for sailing and they're something else, but you, my dear, are running a tad late. Think you can shower, dress and have breakfast in half an hour?'

'Just watch me!'

His lips twisted into a smile. 'I will, with pleasure.'

They had a wonderful day but when they arrived back at their bure after dinner that night they only got as far as the lounge.

Rhiannon wore an apricot silk halter-neck top with a frothy white skirt and high white strappy sandals. She was also wearing her pearls.

She'd tied her hair back and coaxed some wavy tendrils to frame her face—the high humidity was causing her hair to curl slightly.

She put her silver purse on a chair and stretched—eliciting a strange little growl from Lee.

She eyed him, still with her arms stretched upwards, and he crossed the room in two quick strides and backed her against the wall, pinning her arms above her head with his hands.

'What?' she queried.

He wore a white linen shirt with patch pockets and designer jeans. His tan had deepened and his eyes glinted sapphire-blue with dangerous little glints in them.

'Does the Siren's Union have a position on upright sex?'

Rhiannon's eyes widened. 'You mean...' She stopped.

'I mean as in here and now.'

'Well,' she paused, 'I—'

'Like this.' He released her arms, but as they sank to her sides his fingers reached behind her neck and untied the halter-neck and pulled it down, revealing her breasts. 'Because if they don't I'm happy to provide not only a rationale but a demonstration.'

'Right here? Against this wall?'

'Yes,' he said crisply. 'Starting with the rationale,' he drew his hands down her body to her waist, 'I've been dying to do this from the moment we sat down to dinner because every time you moved this blasted flimsy silk,' he took a handful of it and crushed it, 'has afforded me tantalising but *veiled*,' he emphasised the word, 'outlines that made me lose my appetite.'

'That sounds—that doesn't sound good,' she protested.

'It was perfectly good. It just relocated my hunger in a different direction. And I did warn you about the consequences of wearing your pearls in public,' he added.

Her lips curved into a smile. 'I didn't actually notice that you weren't eating.'

'I did go through the motions,' he agreed, 'but not with any great pleasure. Well, that was the rationale, now for the demonstration.'

She closed her hand over his and started to speak but he overrode her.

'Rhiannon,' he growled, 'I don't know if you believe me but I'm going crazy.'

'Maybe this will help,' she said with utter gravity as she removed the top, swiftly released her skirt and kicked it away as it pooled at her feet. And she stood tall and proud in front of him, wearing only a very small pair of stretch-lace bikini briefs, her high-heeled sandals—and her pearls.

He took a breath and a muscle flickered in his jaw as that dark blue gaze tracked her from head to toe. Her ripe breasts with their velvet tips, the translucence of her skin that even challenged her pearls, the slenderness of her waist, her belly button, the tiny triangle of lace of her briefs and the lovely length of her legs.

The most divine tremors started to run through her and she began to flick his shirt buttons open. Then her fingers reached the waist of his jeans and she flipped open the stud and drew down the zip.

From then on, although they never did dispense with his shirt, he tore off the rest of his clothes, she stepped out of her briefs and he picked her up so she could wrap her legs around him and, both almost frantic with desire, he took her there and then.

'This union you belong to,' he said later, when they were lying propped up by pillows on the bed and watching the moon, 'they certainly send you out…fully prepared for all eventualities.'

She smiled dreamily. 'On the contrary, it all comes down to one vital factor.'

'Oh? What's that?' He stroked her hair and dropped a light kiss on the tip of her nose.

'It's the art of choosing a partner, then all you have to do is go with the flow.'

He laughed softly. 'Thanks, but I think it would be fairer to say the effect we have on *each other* is rather spectacular.'

Rhiannon frowned faintly. 'So?'

'I was only hoping you would agree.'

She rolled onto her side so she could face him. She wore a brief turquoise satin nightgown with shoestring straps, he had on a pair of pyjama trousers.

The mosquito net was down and the only light coming into the room was from the lounge. She felt almost as if she was marooned on an island with him, insulated and isolated from the rest of the world.

'Yes, I would agree,' she said eventually.

'So nothing's going to change when we leave here.'

'You mean—this isn't some secret bower with magical properties? A time and place that can't be replicated in the real world?'

He grimaced and slipped some strands of her hair through his fingers. 'Something like that.'

'I guess there has been a fantasy element to it, though, my tall, dark, dangerous pirate,' she said.

'We didn't start out that way,' he pointed out.

'That seems like so long ago.' She looked back through the weeks to the first time they'd slept together in his bedroom. 'Why are you—why are we having this conversation, Lee? I thought—things were sorted between us.'

'I just want them to stay sorted. We're leaving tomorrow. I'm taking you out west for a tour of a couple of cattle stations before we go home. We know your father is doing well and your aunt is there for him anyway.'

'Oh. Well, I can't imagine a cattle station or two is going to change how I feel about you.'

'Good. Ready for sleep?'

She nodded.

He got out of bed to switch the lamp off in the lounge then crawled back in under the net and took her in his arms.

'Mmm,' she murmured drowsily, 'I love this too.'

'Go to sleep,' he said softly.

She did, but when she woke the next morning she was alone and for some reason it brought back their conversation of the previous evening and raised a little question mark in her mind.

Had there been an undertone she didn't understand? Why did she have that unsolved *something* on the edge of her mind again?

Then it occurred to her that her resolve to preserve a part of her Lee Richardson couldn't reach was virtually non-existent now...

She got up and wandered out onto the veranda. The rising sun was spreading a living pink on the water and the mountains on the other side of the estuary were hazy and dusky blue.

There was no one about save for a lone figure standing at the end of the jetty, the jetty they'd fished from—Lee. But he wasn't fishing. He was standing with his hands shoved into the pockets of his shorts, staring straight ahead and obviously deep in thought.

Rhiannon caught her breath as the profound impression struck her that he'd gone away from her to some zone she knew nothing about...

But what really affected her was the stab of pain it brought her, and the realisation that came with it. In four days, hour by hour, Lee Richardson had come to mean more and more to her. Had she fallen hopelessly in love with him? she asked herself.

Even if not that, had she got to a stage where any barriers between them were going to hurt her?

CHAPTER SIX

A WEEK later her fears had subsided.

They'd travelled via a variety of transport from helicopters and light planes to dusty trucks over hundreds of miles of outback country.

They'd stayed at station homesteads, including the one Lee had grown up on, Jindalee. She'd participated, on horseback, in a cattle muster and shown an aptitude for it.

She'd camped out with Lee under the stars beside a billabong and loved every minute of it.

As well as all that, she gained new insights into the man she'd married. Dressed in a bush shirt, jeans and dusty boots with a 'fair dinkum' broad-brimmed cattleman's felt hat, he was very much at home doing everything his employees did.

But under the easy familiarity that was the way of the outback, there was no mistaking who was the boss, no mistaking the keen mind that saw the big picture and held it all together.

There were also times, when she watched him on his horse, the reins in one hand, riding knees and heels, wheeling and wielding a stock whip, that did strange things to the pit of her stomach and made her ever more receptive to his lovemaking.

It was a strange sensation being married to a man you had almost a girlish crush on, she decided.

Everywhere they'd gone, they'd been greeted with enthusiasm. Apparently it was a source of satisfaction for all his employees that Lee Richardson had tied the knot at last, and not only that, but also to a girl who could ride like the wind. A girl who didn't mind getting dusty and dirty, was a whiz in the kitchen and also scrubbed up rather dishily.

'You've taken everyone by storm, Rhiannon,' Lee said to her one afternoon. 'Anyone would think you were born to this kind of life.'

'Far from it.' She grimaced.

They were out riding but just for pleasure. There was a particularly spectacular waterhole he'd said he wanted to show her—it was on Jindalee—one he'd swum in most of his life.

They wore their swimming things under their clothes and it was bakingly hot as they rode through the bush with its lovely colours of ochre soil, sage-green grass and an unlimited blue sky.

'Here we are.' He reined in and dismounted. She did the same.

'Oh, wow!' she breathed as she looked around.

The waterhole was in a bend of a sandy creek bed and surrounded by huge old ghost gums dispensing dappled shade and home to a flock of pink and white galahs that took to the air, squawking, then settled back again.

'This is so beautiful! Race you into the water,' she challenged.

They hit the pool at the same time and the spray rose into the air.

'It's cold,' she carolled in surprise.

'I know. Comes from an underground spring. See that old rope up there?' He pointed to a branch that leaned across the creek.

'Yes!'

'That was my idea. We used to climb the tree and swing over and plunge into the pool from it.'

'We?'

'Matt and I and all the station kids—maybe they still do but it might be an idea to check it out, it looks a bit old and tatty.'

Rhiannon swam up to him. 'I think it would be a very good idea. So you were a real daredevil even as a little boy?'

'No more than most. What kind of a little girl were you?'

She considered. 'A right handful so I've been told—and retold only recently, as it happens.'

He put his arms around her. 'When?'

'Uh—I think I'll maintain a diplomatic silence on that one.'

'Then—how's this for diplomacy? I can believe it but you're also such a *gorgeous* handful it's hard to mind.' And he moved his hands on her body.

'I haven't done anything to make you believe it,' she protested, 'but—that is nice.'

'It could get a lot nicer,' he murmured and took off her bikini top.

'You make quite a habit of doing that,' she remonstrated but negated the effect by lying back across his arms and wrapping her legs around him.

'So do you—of this.'

She sat up. 'Mind? It is a rather favoured position of mine.'

'Nope. I—' But he stopped as a bellow split the air and they turned convulsively to see a mob of cattle on the far bank, eyeing them.

'Holy cow!' Rhiannon said, employing an irreverent but apt form of address. 'I thought we were alone! That puts a different complexion on things.'

'It does?'

'Yes, definitely. Wouldn't you agree?'

'Yes,' he said but he was shaking with laughter. Then he kissed her and presently they climbed out of the pool and dried themselves and Lee produced a Thermos, two metal cups and a container out of his saddlebag.

They got dressed and sat on their towels, drinking their tea, chatting idly and waving away the little bush flies. The cattle had drunk and dispersed.

'Do you ever feel torn between this and city life, Lee?' she asked. 'Not that Southall is exactly city.'

'Sometimes,' he admitted. 'But I always spend a couple of months a year up here.'

'You know,' she confided, 'right from the beginning I got the feeling there was more to you than a boardroom suit. How's that for perspicacity or feminine intuition?'

'What gave you that idea?'

'I'm not sure. Anyway, it must have been a great place to grow up.'

'It had a lot going for it. Funnily enough, bush kids often hanker for the big smoke but I guess I had the best of both worlds. Boarding-school on the Gold Coast then uni in Brisbane, and, of course, Southall. Where would you like our kids to grow up, Rhiannon?'

She was about to pop a bit of biscuit in her mouth but she froze, then put it down. 'I haven't thought about that.'

'Is there any reason not to?'

She swallowed some tea. 'No but we've only been married for a week or so.'

He stretched out his legs and lay back on his elbow. 'Is there any hang-up to do with your miscarriage?'

She stared at him. 'No. No physical impediment—it was just one of those pregnancies destined to terminate, so I was told.'

'But it devastated you?' he queried quietly.

'It—did. It was hard to work out why, though, after being rejected by the—the father.'

'Were you wildly in love with him?'

She said with an effort, 'I thought so at the time. With the benefit of hindsight, the fact that everything was crashing down round my ears may have coloured things oddly for me.' She looked away.

'I'm sure it can happen.'

She sniffed and finished her biscuit. 'Strangely, though, you know what was the most devastating? The fact that it was *my* baby I lost. It was—such a lonely feeling.' She wiped a tear off her cheek.

Lee sat up abruptly and put his arms around her. He didn't say anything but his warmth and bulk were wonderfully comforting.

She raised her head at last. 'Anyway, that's all in the past now.'

'Yes.' He brushed some strands of hair out of her eyes and looked deeply into them. 'Have you any idea how much I admire you?'

Her lips parted.

'Oh, yes,' he said. 'Listen, shall we go home tomorrow? I have a few commitments.'

* * *

There was a surprise waiting for them at Southall.

They got home after dark, to see lights on in the house. 'Probably Matt and Mary come up for the weekend,' Lee said as he opened the front door and dumped their bags in the hall. 'Shouldn't I carry you over the doorstep?'

'Oh, I'll step outside again,' Rhiannon offered but they both paused at the sound of footsteps. It was neither Matt nor Mary, however, who walked into the hall; it was Andrea.

Andrea, with that provocative walk and her river of dark, glossy hair flowing down her back, wearing white hipster trousers and a tangerine silk shirt.

Lee said, 'Andrea?' with patent disbelief.

'Why, Lee,' she replied in her fascinatingly husky voice, 'I was wondering when you'd come home. Rhiannon, congratulations! I think this calls for some champagne, don't you?'

'Thank you,' Rhiannon heard herself say into the electric silence. She moved forward and offered her hand to the other girl.

Andrea Richardson hesitated then put her hand into Rhiannon's as she swept Rhiannon from head to toe with a critical glance from her long-lashed great dark eyes.

Rhiannon didn't flinch, although in contrast to Andrea she wasn't exactly looking *soignée* in jeans, boots and a denim jacket.

But, while she hadn't expected a warm response from Lee's stepmother, she was somewhat taken aback by the sheer hostility that was beamed her way for an instant before Andrea veiled her eyes and murmured a cool, 'Welcome to the family.'

'As a matter of interest, what are you doing at

Southall, Andrea?' Lee queried, and Rhiannon could sense the tension in him.

Andrea smiled, a sleepy, tantalising little smile. 'Have you forgotten about the memorial service I'm organising for your father, Lee?'

'No, but I thought it was at least a month away.'

'I've brought it forward—it's in two weeks' time so it makes sense for me to be here, since it's to be held in the local church and then the reception here at Southall, don't you agree? I was his wife whether you like it or not,' she added gently.

Rhiannon heard Lee's swift intake of breath and something prompted her to intervene.

'Andrea,' she said serenely, 'of course you're welcome and I do hope you've made yourself comfortable. Just give us a moment or two to shake the dust out of our hair, will you? We are a bit travel-stained but then we'd love to share a toast with you. Come, darling,' she added to Lee.

'Well done,' Lee said and took Rhiannon in his arms after he'd closed them into his wing.

She grimaced. 'Maybe not so well done if you mean the "lady of the manor" pose I took. I get the feeling I've made an enemy for life.'

'She wasn't going to take kindly to whoever kept her out of Southall,' he said, and rested his chin on the top of her head for a moment. 'But in you she may just realise she's met her match. Listen,' he moved Rhiannon away so he could look into her eyes, 'do you mind moving in here with me for the time being?'

Rhiannon blinked. 'Not at all. Why?'

'I took the opportunity to renovate the master suite while we were away...new bathroom et cetera. It's not finished yet—and you can redecorate it to your heart's content.'

'Thanks.' Her lips curved into a smile. 'I'd like that, although I'm just as happy with a tent.'

He grinned and kissed her lightly. 'I might hold you to that one day. Why don't you have a shower before continuing your lady-of-the-manor role?'

But Rhiannon hesitated. 'This is really difficult for you, isn't it, Lee?'

He sobered. 'Yes. I was…very fond of my father and, although I may have given off indications to the contrary, I do understand that she struck at what was a difficult time for him. So,' he paused and frowned, 'I didn't want to break up the family but I *don't* want her here.'

'Why are you so sure she's a gold-digger?' Rhiannon asked with a frown of her own.

'He would have been sixty this year, she's thirty-two, Rhiannon,' he said deliberately. 'If that isn't enough, she got him to marry her without either Matt or myself knowing what was happening or being able to preach caution. And afterwards, it was the last thing he was going to want to hear.'

Rhiannon sighed. 'I guess that does damn her a bit but I might take another tack.'

He gazed at her narrowly. 'Such as?'

Rhiannon shrugged. 'I'll just be friendly. We've got to get through this memorial service somehow, anyway.'

He continued to gaze at her intently. 'I guess so. Just watch yourself.'

Rhiannon blinked. 'There's nothing she can do to me,' she said.

'Yes, there is.' He paused, a long, curiously tense

pause, with the lines and angles of his face setting in stone. Then he drew a deep breath. 'We were lovers before she married my father.'

Rhiannon's lips parted soundlessly and the room seemed to whirl a little around her. She closed her eyes, but when she opened them experimentally everything was back in place, the lovely paintings on the walls, the chess set on the coffee-table...

But the last piece of the jigsaw, that unsolved *something*, had also fallen into place.

She should have realised from the moment she'd known what lengths Lee was prepared to go to, to keep his stepmother out of Southall, that the reason for it had to be *this*...

'He had no idea,' Lee continued in that same hard voice. 'She lived in Sydney and it was a slightly long-distance affair. Matt didn't know either. We broke it off when she found I wasn't amenable to being manipulated—that I expected her to live my kind of life, cattle stations in other words, not the other way around. You could say she paid me back handsomely. I went away to Argentina for two months, mostly cattle business. When I came back she'd married my father.

'She then proceeded to demonstrate just how successful she was at twisting him round her little finger, even to the extent of getting him to move to France.'

'Lee,' Rhiannon whispered, 'so she's the reason you got turned off commitment?' As if I don't know now, she taunted herself.

He nodded.

'You should have told me!'

'I'm telling you now, Rhiannon. The only difference from what I told you before is that you can put a name and a face to it now.'

'It's not the only difference,' she said urgently. 'I assumed it was all over and done with. I had no idea I would be…paraded in front of an ex-lover in a…in a what's-sauce-for-the-goose-is-sauce-for-the-gander scenario!' She broke off frustratedly. 'That doesn't say it perfectly but you must know what I mean, a *see if I care* scenario.'

'It's nothing like that at all,' he denied roughly.

'It's over and done with—do you honestly imagine I could cherish any form of finer feelings for a woman who did what she did?'

'I don't think those kind of feelings are always susceptible to what one *should* or should *not* do.'

'Nonsense,' he said sharply. 'Look,' he took hold, 'to be perfectly honest I'd rather nobody knew. It's the kind of nightmare situation you hope to hell you never have to divulge. That's why…' He stopped and shrugged. 'That's why I didn't. Can you understand that, Rhiannon? He was my *father*.'

She stared at him, pale to her lips. 'Well, maybe, but in that case, why are you telling me now?'

'The thought of you trying to befriend her—' he stopped frustratedly '—suddenly brought to mind the fact that it could be a perfect tool for her to undermine *us*.'

'You mean Andrea wouldn't be above telling me what you've just told me?'

'Perhaps not. She's already taken one possibility to get back at me and turned it into a reality.'

'How about—wanting you back?' Rhiannon asked, wide-eyed and paler than pale now.

'She hasn't got a chance in hell,' he said grimly. 'She knows that but I wouldn't put it past her to try to create maximum damage between us,' he added cynically. 'But look, we both knew we had experiences behind us that were unhappy and had changed us. Didn't we?'

'All the same—no.' She stopped abruptly and closed her eyes briefly. 'I can't think straight but yes, I guess we have,' she said bleakly and added, 'Did you intend to tell me at all? I mean, if she hadn't turned up?'

'Yes. I always knew she'd turn up sooner or later.'

'But you decided to wait until I was so—hooked, it mightn't have made a difference?' she challenged.

'What do you mean?'

Her mind flew back to the conversation they'd had the day before. 'I mean pregnant, maybe, not to mention indebted to you over my father—I am that already, although at least I still have a chance to repay you there, so—'

'No,' he said harshly and his fingers closed over her wrist. 'I was hoping things would have fallen into place for us so completely it wouldn't matter a row of beans. Incidentally, nothing's changed my mind to the contrary. I see no reason why they can't. Do you?'

Rhiannon stared up at him and jumped as the house phone rang.

He reached for it impatiently. 'Yes, what is it?' he barked down the line, not taking his eyes from Rhiannon's face.

She couldn't tell the gist of the conversation from his monosyllables but he was clearly pressured when he put the phone down.

'That was Matt. Mary's been put into hospital with some virus they can't identify so they're taking no chances. Matt, understandably, wants to be with her but he's due at an important conference tomorrow in Melbourne and he's asked me to take his place—I'm

the only one who can. Andrea is going down to see
Mary now. I'll have to leave tonight too in order to get
the first flight tomorrow.'

'You do understand, don't you?' he said later. 'Although
why the hell you won't come with me is—'

'No, Lee,' Rhiannon said firmly as she helped him
pack a bag. For some reason it had become paramount
to her not to walk into yet another wall of Lee's
making. 'Don't forget I haven't seen my father for
nearly two weeks now, so I *must* do it.'

'One condition, then—otherwise I'll put a halter
on you.' He smiled fleetingly but not with particular
amusement. 'You don't allow Andrea to come between
us in your thoughts—in other words you don't do
anything silly until I get back.'

She studied him coolly. 'That's not a good choice
of words, Lee.'

'Maybe not,' he conceded, 'but think of the
Bloomfield and how we made love, because that's
what I'll be thinking of. And missing you.'

He took the pile of shirts out of her hand and tossed
them on the bed so he could take her in his arms.
'Missing you like hell,' he said barely audibly, 'and
this.'

He started to kiss her. She tried not to respond but
he was too clever for her. He knew exactly how she
liked it now and all the right buttons to push so that
when he drew away she was shaken to the core with
desire and horrified at the thought of being left alone.

He observed the pulse fluttering wildly at the base
of her throat and shadows in her eyes. 'Will you change
your mind?'

It was with the greatest effort of will that she said, 'No. But I'll…miss you too.'

Something flickered in his eyes but she couldn't identify it and all he said was, 'OK. Take care of yourself.' Then he went on to practicalities.

He told there was a mare in the stables she might like to ride, and since it was school holidays she might like to take Christy with her. He suggested, with a wicked little grin, that she might also like to do a bit of horse whispering with Poppy. He said if she needed to access her emails to use his computer in the library.

He told her the blue Mercedes station wagon was now hers and he handed her a brand-new credit card in the name of Mrs Rhiannon Richardson. The limit on it made her eyes widen, it was so large.

She hesitated then agreed to everything, although what she really felt like telling him was that she felt "bought", but it wasn't the time or place, and it probably wasn't the correct sentiment anyway—more of a case that she'd sold herself…

Rhiannon closed the front door on Lee and looked around. The house was suddenly huge and silent, almost scarily so. She swallowed then she reminded herself that Cliff and Christy were in the gardener's cottage only a few hundred yards from the house, and she relaxed a little.

She had a shower then made herself a light supper before, with a heartfelt yawn, taking herself to bed in Lee's wing.

But sleep was hard to come by.

It was a bed that held some momentous memories for her and despite fresh bedlinen, Lee's presence was almost tangible, so much so, it was hard to crystallise her dilemma against the power of those memories.

Obviously an experience such as his had to have made him cynical and more so than just a love affair turned sour involving just the two of them.

But if there was a secret hankering for Andrea he couldn't quite kill despite denying it so strenuously, it was worse—much worse.

It meant there *was* another zone he retreated to, as she'd sensed in their last morning on the Bloomfield, possibly even a private little hell for him.

It meant no other woman would get anything but the crumbs...

She turned her head on the pillow and grimaced. Pretty spectacular crumbs—her father taken care of, luxury, wonderful sex, but never the real core of the man, and to think that was what she had been afraid of revealing!

No, she thought despairingly then. Maybe he's right, maybe it is all over for him, it was a terrible thing to do—marry his father to get back at him.

So why did she have this—this intuition, she asked herself, that the attraction between them wasn't completely smashed to pieces? Because he'd been so determined to keep Andrea out of Southall, even to the extent of marrying a virtual stranger because he could never forgive her? But if he could never forgive her, was the hurt still there? And if the hurt was still there...

She moved restlessly and transferred her thoughts to her own feelings.

If their marriage had been a union between two scarred people, both genuinely not capable of falling in love, then time, the respect they shared, plus the attraction between them, might have secured it.

If one of them had fallen madly in love, however, that was another matter altogether.

She grimaced as she thought that thought and wondered who she was trying to kid with a clinical summation of the facts that sounded as if it had come out of a textbook.

She had fallen in love with him—there was nothing clinical about the level of hurt she was experiencing to think that he hadn't respected her or trusted her enough to tell her his innermost secret. Nothing clinical at all to imagine him with another woman she now knew in the flesh—and feel like screaming...

Was that why, she wondered suddenly, he'd introduced a fantasy element to their married life? Not only to help her over her own difficulties but also to remove it to another plane that Andrea Richardson had no part in?

It was a bizarre thought but it troubled her obscurely and she thought back to their last conversation the night before they left the Bloomfield after they'd participated in sizzling upright sex.

She'd had the strange feeling at the time that there was an undercurrent she'd missed. Was it his way of warning her that she might find herself on shaky ground one day, so hang on to these moments?

She shook her head frustratedly and finally fell into a fitful sleep. Once, when she woke up, she cursed herself for refusing to go with Lee. Anything would have been better than lying alone and greatly fearful in his bed...

CHAPTER SEVEN

LEE rang her early the next morning with a surprise request.

He told her that Mary was resting fairly comfortably but her condition was still a bit of a mystery, so Matt and Andrea were staying in Brisbane. Then,

'I know this is a bit like history repeating itself and dreadfully short notice, but I could be gone for a couple of days and it might—you might appreciate something to do,' he said down the line. 'Get the house ready for the memorial service.'

'Me?'

'Look, I'm sorry,' he said intensely, 'but there's no way of putting it off now Andrea has spread the word and—it is the kind of thing you do superbly. I also, for my father's sake, would like it to be a genuine and moving celebration of his life. There will also be pretty important people attending—at least one state premier.'

'Of course,' Rhiannon said quietly. 'What does Andrea have to say, though?'

'At least she's been fairly organised but the house and the caterers she's happy to leave up to you. And not only are you superb at it but it is your home,

Rhiannon. Make that our home. One thing, though, do get in caterers. I don't want you working your fingers to the bone and I'm sure there'll be quite a crowd.'

'I'll do my best. How's Melbourne?'

'Funnily enough, it reminds me of the day four years ago when I met you.'

'It's pouring?' she hazarded.

'Proverbial cats and dogs. How are you?'

'I'm fine. And, you're right, it will give me something to do.'

'All right. Listen, what are you wearing?'

'I—' Rhiannon looked down at herself '—jeans and a jumper, it's a bit chilly.'

'No pearls?'

'No. Why?'

'Pity. I might have had to put myself on the first plane home.'

Rhiannon couldn't help laughing softly and they talked for a few minutes more with no constraints until he told her his flight had been called.

She drove down to see her father and aunt that morning.

Before Lee's call she'd primed herself to put on the greatest act of her life for her aunt and father, a glowing-bride act rather than the confused, unhappy person she'd become overnight.

But after their conversation, she couldn't help feeling somewhat reassured.

Then the fact that Luke Fairfax was doing so well also helped. He was allowed up in a wheelchair and, although it was going to take extensive physio and other therapy to get him on his feet, he was cheerful— he was even playing his guitar and giving little impromptu concerts for other patients.

Both he and Di enjoyed Rhiannon's descriptions of her honeymoon and they both accepted without question the fact that she'd be really tied up over the next few days.

She drove back to Southall in quite a positive frame of mind.

Two days later, while Lee was still in Melbourne, Andrea came to lunch.

She'd rung the day before to make sure it was convenient for Rhiannon, who had decided not to mention it to Lee in their phone conversations, and she arrived bearing a bottle of champagne wrapped and beribboned in gold foil paper and an orchid in a pot similarly wrapped.

'Why, thank you!' Rhiannon said. She'd taken some care with her appearance. She'd put on a fitted short-sleeved dress in a summery blue stretch fabric dotted with mauve flowers, and high blue sandals. She was lightly made up and her hair was smooth and shining and she was wearing her pearls.

'We never did get to drink a toast,' Andrea said. 'And orchids are supposed to last for ever.'

'Are they? How's Mary?' Rhiannon asked as she led the way to the veranda, where she'd set up a lunch table with a beautifully appliquéd cloth, the Flora Dora Mikasa china with its narrow black and gold rim and pink rosebuds, and some real pink rosebuds in a silver loving cup.

It was a lovely day, there were birds singing in the garden and dragonflies hovering in the clear air.

'They're letting her go home tomorrow. All the tests for anything nasty that could affect the baby have been negative—they now think it was just a touch of flu.'

'That's good news.' There was an open bottle of wine set in a silver cooler on the table.

Rhiannon poured two glasses after a questioning look at Andrea, and they sat down. Sharon brought out the casserole Rhiannon had made of pork cutlets with an apple and cream sauce.

'So,' Rhiannon said after she'd served them, 'you said we needed to talk. If you'd like to be more involved in the catering and so forth for the memorial service, that's fine with me, Andrea.'

'No, I wouldn't.' Andrea lifted her knife and fork. She wore slim cream linen trousers and gauzy grey and yellow blouse. 'I have it on the evidence of my own eyes that you're the person who can handle it best.'

'Then?'

'There's no reason we can't get to know each other a little, is there?'

'Probably not but you sounded rather serious.'

Andrea ate thoughtfully for a while, then, 'Unless you are prepared to accept the view that I am the wicked stepmother.'

Rhiannon considered for a moment. 'No, I'm not. Things can happen between men and women that don't make a lot of sense to others but they happen all the same. I do also think that men find it harder to cope when they lose a partner, in general—that's why they often remarry or get into another relationship fairly soon. My own father is an exception, as it happens, but,' she shrugged, 'what was between you and Lee's father has nothing to do with me.'

Andrea stared at her as if she was making some judgements of her own. Finally she said, 'Do you have any idea what it's like to be treated as an outcast?'

Rhiannon looked away. 'Andrea, this really has nothing to do with me. I— Anyway—'

'Do you have any idea what it's like being accused of shortening Ross's life?'

Rhiannon looked shocked. 'They haven't said that, surely!'

'No, but I'm sure Lee's thought it, despite the fact that Ross had rheumatic fever as a child, which affected his heart, and he often joked that he never thought he'd make fifty, let alone sixty.'

'He has, Lee—I mean, he allowed you to hold this memorial service,' Rhiannon said carefully.

'He couldn't stop me.' Andrea's dark eyes flashed. 'Don't think I don't know that I'll be relegated as soon as it's over, though. But I'm not prepared to accept it and I want you to tell him that.'

'Why me?' Rhiannon looked astounded.

'It was a choice of you or Matt, to be honest. He's never been quite as anti me as Lee. As for Lee himself, beyond absolute banalities, he's like a brick wall. He even refuses, unless it's absolutely necessary, to be in the same room with me.'

Rhiannon opened her mouth to say she knew the brick-wall feeling but stopped herself in time. And she suddenly remembered Mary's party and Lee's insistence that she go as a guest—after he'd realised Andrea was to be a guest too? To counteract Andrea's presence? she wondered now. That probably made more sense than her social skills…

'I think Matt would have been a better bet,' she said slowly. 'I'm so—new to the family.'

'All the same, you must have some—' Andrea smiled sketchily '—you must have some influence over Lee. That's why I'd like you to tell him. As well as telling him he may think he can ignore me—'

'But,' Rhiannon interjected, and stopped abruptly.

'I made his father very happy over the last years of his life whatever Lee might like to think, so there *has* to be a place for me.'

Rhiannon blinked several times as she grappled with the issue.

Andrea pushed her plate away, half-finished. 'I'm sorry, it's delicious, but I don't seem to have much appetite. And I'm sorry to dump this on you, Rhiannon, but Lee has given me no choice. So would you please tell him that unless he sees things my way, I'm fully prepared to air some of the family's dirty linen in public. He'll know what I mean.'

No choice? Rhiannon thought as she held Andrea's dark gaze steadily. *I find that hard to believe, so why are you doing this, Andrea?*

To make sure *I* know what happened just in case Lee has left me in ignorance? If so, that means you have another agenda, Andrea... Could it be in the nature of throwing a spanner in the works between me and Lee?

She rubbed the bridge of her nose and said abruptly, 'I'll think about it. But I won't be doing anything until after the memorial—and neither should you,' she said definitely.

Andrea lifted a dark eyebrow. 'Not just a pretty face?' she hazarded.

'No,' Rhiannon agreed coolly and composedly.

'Very well.' Andrea shrugged and finished her wine. 'I must say, you do seem to be particularly competent.'

Rhiannon let that one pass.

'But for what it's worth, I did make Ross happy,' Andrea continued. 'Yes, I may have married him on the rebound but he knew that, although not who it was. He also knew I was on my uppers at the time and,' she gestured a little frustratedly, 'I'm not good at handling that.'

Rhiannon said nothing.

'But he was kind and thoughtful, he was—' Andrea stopped to dash at a couple of tears '—after all the drama that had gone before he was…wonderful. You can believe it or not,' she said hoarsely and pulled a hanky from her pocket to blow her nose, 'but it's the truth.'

A sterling performance, Rhiannon found herself wondering, or the truth? But what about the gaps? Such as the convenient glossing over of who the man she'd been on the rebound from was…

And why was Lee refusing even to be in the same room as Andrea unless absolutely necessary—because he didn't trust himself?

Andrea left not long afterwards, which was probably just as well because Lee arrived home looking tired and ill.

'Oh, I wasn't expecting you,' Rhiannon greeted him, and frowned immediately. 'What's wrong?'

'I don't know, I just feel whacked. You may not realise it, but it's a great strain being away from you, Mrs Richardson.'

Rhiannon felt her heart melt as she looked into his blue eyes, and everything else, including his manipulative stepmother, fled from her mind.

She took his hand and said softly, 'Come.' And she led him to his wing.

He closed the door behind them with one hand and took off his tie with other, and pulled her into his arms without saying a word.

She didn't speak either, just rested against him with

her arms wound round him. Then she took his hand again and led him to the bed.

'Is this what I think it is?' he queried.

She only smiled serenely and started to undress quite naturally and undramatically.

She was down to her underwear, a black bra and black lacy knickers, her pearls and with her shiny fair hair covering her face as she bent down to slide her knickers off when he moved convulsively and said hoarsely, 'I don't know if this is what you had in mind, but I don't think I can help myself.'

And his hands were hard on her body as he ripped her bra off, shed his clothes and claimed her.

There was no teasing her nipples with champagne, no sensuous massage of her hips, nothing but naked, rampant need until he shuddered over her.

'I'm sorry, I'm sorry,' he said harshly as he rolled off her and took her in his arms. 'That was un—'

'No,' she said softly.

'But I didn't even give you time to respond!'

'There'll be other times,' she murmured. 'I just thought you might be in great need of some kind of—release.'

'You thought right. I don't know what's the matter with me…' He shrugged. 'How's your father?'

She told him. And she told him about the arrangements she'd been putting in place for the reception after the memorial service.

'Well, I think I may have to leave you for the moment,' she said then.

'Why? This is very—pleasant.' He cuddled her against him then chuckled softly.

'What?'

'I never saw myself as a cuddler but you bring a

whole new meaning to the word. You have just the right curves for it.' He paid particular attention to some of those curves.

'That is going beyond cuddling,' she pointed out on an indrawn breath. 'So I'm going to have to take a rain check.'

'Are you sure?' He reached for her but she slipped off the bed.

'I'm—sure it's in everyone's interests in the long term. You look as if you could do with a breather and I have an appointment with the caterers in,' she looked at the bedside clock and groaned, 'twenty minutes!'

'You know you wouldn't get away with this if it weren't for the caterers, Rhiannon?'

'Yes, probably, although don't always expect to get your own way!' She waved to him and went into the shower.

When she came out, he was fast asleep. She looked her fill for a long moment then tiptoed around getting dressed.

Lee slept through it all and she tiptoed out, blowing him a kiss.

In fact he slept on and off through to quite late the next morning. She started to wonder whether she should call a doctor, but when she went to suggest it she found him awake and looking much better.

'I think you may have had some kind of a bug; maybe the one Mary had is doing the rounds,' she said, sitting down beside him.

'I think you're right. I started to feel crook almost as soon as I arrived in Melbourne. So.' He sat up. 'What orders have you got for me?'

'None. Everything's under control but your fax machine has been going ballistic—I borrowed your desk in the library and I did check my email on your computer…none for me but your inbox is overflowing.'

He grimaced. 'George, no doubt. We're considering an offer for a station in WA and he's always meticulous about clearing the last detail with me. OK.' He got up and pulled on a tracksuit. 'There's something I want to show you. A room.'

'What room?'

'You'll see.'

It was his mother's study he led her to.

Not large, it overlooked the rose garden and had a cosy air with a chintz-covered couch, pretty paintings on the walls, family photos in silver frames and a roll-top desk.

'She used to say it was her "command module",' he explained. 'She used to keep all the household records as well as extensive records of all her entertaining in this desk—you may find them useful, and there's both an outside line and an internal phone and we'll get you a computer. It's all yours to command now, Mrs Richardson,' he added gravely.

'Thank you,' Rhiannon responded, a little awestruck for a moment.

Lee pulled open a desk drawer and revealed monogrammed stationery. He picked up a sheet. 'Margaret Richardson,' he said quietly. 'Now, she was a lady.'

'Lee,' Rhiannon breathed, 'I think men are worse at—coping with being on their own than women. And—maybe it's time to bury the hatchet with Andrea?'

'Perhaps.' He shrugged. 'You'll need to order

yourself your own stationery. OK.' He closed the drawer. 'Meet me at the pool at, say, five-thirty?'

Rhiannon agreed.

But after he'd gone, she sat down in the swivel chair at the desk and pondered things such as—could it be that Lee's burying of the hatchet towards his stepmother would only ever be skin-deep?

Such as, *did* Andrea Richardson deserve a place in the family after the mayhem she'd caused? Come to that, was she hell-bent on causing more mayhem? But what kind of mayhem could she cause? She didn't know it but the dirty linen wouldn't come as a surprise to Lee's new wife...

Rhiannon shook her head and contemplated another dilemma to do with how she'd almost instinctively buried all her concerns and would do so until after the memorial—what else could she do? she wondered.

And in the meantime she had plenty to concentrate on if she wanted Southall to look its best.

Margaret Richardson's records proved a godsend.

From them she hired an army of cleaners to tackle the windows, walls, floors, carpets, upholstery and the silver. She found several tradesmen for the little things she'd noticed, like a couple of leaking taps, some cracked flagging in the entrance courtyard and some small painting jobs.

All of them were prepared to fit Southall into their busy schedules.

At Ross Richardson's memorial service, Rhiannon felt as if the last days had been fast-forwarded.

Somehow she'd maintained her unaffected air—as if she had no idea her husband and his stepmother had

had an affair before Andrea had married Ross on the
rebound. As if she were unaware of the drama sure to
unfold when Andrea staked her claim.

Talk about a sterling performance, she had thought
once—she was the one who deserved an Oscar.

But the fact that both she and Lee had been so busy
had helped. The fact that every guest bedroom at
Southall, and there were eight, had gradually filled
with long-term, interstate friends of the family gave her
more than enough to do on top of what she was already
doing, and she often fell into bed exhausted.

'We'll take a break after this is over,' Lee had said
to her one night when he slid into bed beside her and
slid his arms around her.

'Mmmm…' she murmured sleepily but not sure she
would sleep.

'How about a distant shore?'

'Yes, nice.'

'Only nice?' he queried offendedly.

'Make that too nice.'

'That's better. Rhiannon, I can't thank you enough
for all you're doing.'

'I can think of one way—just hold me until I fall
asleep. I'm a bit over-the-top, I think.'

'Done. Sweet dreams.'

She came back to the present, standing beside Lee in
the flower-filled church. The service was nearly ended
and it had been moving but uplifting.

The music had been lovely and the speakers
inspired, especially Lee's eulogy, a blend of humour,
admiration and respect, that had brought his father to
life for the congregation. And the final musical piece
was the mysterious notes of a didgeridoo to highlight

Ross Richardson's connection with the outback and its traditions.

Rhiannon broke out in goose pimples as those deep notes lingered on the air—Lee's choice.

She glanced at Andrea, wearing navy and cream and a marvellous broad-brimmed hat, but could tell nothing from her expression.

Then they were moving down the aisle, Andrea first, she and Lee then Matt and Mary, and out into the sunshine, where the long line of introductions began, made somewhat complicated by the fact that few knew Lee had married.

'Well, well,' one prominent politician said as he shook Rhiannon's hand and took in her charcoal silk suit worn with her pearls and a ruby straw pillbox hat perched on her shiny fair hair—not to mention the figure and legs beneath it, 'I always knew you had great taste, Lee, me boy! I would say you've married yourself a peach.'

'Thank you,' Lee replied gravely. 'I happen to be in agreement. What's wrong?' he added to Rhiannon almost beneath his breath as she moved restlessly. 'He may not be a model of tact but he means well.'

'Yes, I guess so. Nothing! I'm fine.' She put out her hand to the next in the line-up.

But she suddenly knew she was not fine. She'd held herself together against the weight of deep uncertainties for too long.

She'd played several parts that were all a farce. She'd contrived to let Lee feel she was prepared to put his past with Andrea away as if it hadn't happened. She'd pretended not to know what Andrea had meant about the family dirty linen.

And she was, here and now, allowing virtually the

rest of the world to know her as Lee's wife when she was unsure she could remain so caught in the crossfire between two people who'd once loved each other.

Not only that, she thought shakily, but also the pain of not knowing whether she'd always be a "suitable" wife rather than a beloved one.

Then the line ended and Lee put her in his car and drove her back to Southall, where he led her straight to the bar and poured her a small brandy.

'Now,' he said as she took a grateful sip, 'what is it?'

She closed her eyes briefly but once again it wasn't the time or place to tell him the truth. She took another sip and called on herself for one more supreme effort.

'I think I may have just done too much lately and—'

He swore but she put her hand on his arm. 'And I was thinking of my mother.' It wasn't a lie—she had thought of her mother during the service, it just wasn't the whole truth.

'I'm sorry,' he said compassionately. 'I guess I've tended to think only of myself lately but—'

'That's natural,' Rhiannon interrupted.

He studied her and saw the lines of strain in her face where usually there were none, and cursed himself. 'Why don't you—we—?' He broke off frustratedly as people began to arrive.

'I'll be fine,' she assured him. 'I know I can do this.' She drained the glass and set it back on the bar and smiled at him. 'Let's go.'

The last straw that broke the camel's back was a look.

Only a look but one of such intensity between two people, Rhiannon was almost destroyed by it.

As wakes tended to do, and probably were intended to do, a relaxation after the service set in as the delicious food and best wines flowed. And many people told her that Southall had never looked so beautiful.

All the same, she nearly missed that devastating look.

If she hadn't decided to go and powder her nose she wouldn't have observed Lee and Andrea pass each other in the passage that led to Lee's wing.

She wouldn't have seen them, unseen herself, stop with a couple of feet between them, and simply stare at each other with palpable tension stamped into every line of their bodies as if there was an almost unbearable longing and hunger flowing between them.

She saw the way Lee's gaze roamed over Andrea—she'd taken off her hat and that wonderful hair was loose and shining like rough silk down her back—she saw the way Andrea accepted his wandering gaze with her head held high but her hands clenching in a way that told its own tale.

She thought, with such a stab of inward pain she nearly cried out, that Lee had looked at her in a lot of ways but never like that, never, almost, as if his life depended on drinking her image in.

She turned away silently, waited a few moments then looked again, but they'd gone into the main lounge.

She did go on to Lee's wing then, where she packed her essentials, and where she left her pearls in their box with a note tucked under them, on her pillow.

She also changed and, using the veranda exit, made her way swiftly to the garage. Fortunately, the driveway had been left clear so she was able to drive the blue Mercedes away with no difficulty, except, that was, for the tears pouring down her cheeks.

CHAPTER EIGHT

SHE was halfway down the windy Mount Tamborine-Nerang road when she noticed a police car parked in a lay-by ahead of her, then a policeman signalling her to pull in.

She all but pounded the steering wheel. The last thing she needed was to be breathalysed at the moment—not that she had anything to worry about on the alcohol front. One small brandy consumed several hours ago and nothing since wasn't going to take her over the legal limit. She was in such a fever to get away that any delay was supremely frustrating.

She'd already had to stop to put petrol in the car when she'd noticed the warning light on the fuel gauge blinking.

She pulled in and wound down the window, and observed that the policeman didn't have any breathalysing equipment in his hands. Had she been speeding? she wondered? And driven past a concealed radar trap?

She opened her mouth but the policeman said, 'Mrs Richardson? Mrs Rhiannon Richardson?'

'I— Yes, but how did you know?'

He was a tall man, about Lee's age, with an open face, but he ignored her question and waved at the police car.

A policewoman got out and came slowly over to the Mercedes, talking into a mobile phone at the same time. She ended the call as she arrived at the window.

'Ma'am, may I introduce my colleague, Senior Constable Laura Givens? And I'm Sergeant Jim Daley.'

'I— How do you do?' Rhiannon said feverishly.

'Ma'am,' the sergeant continued, 'we're just conducting some routine safety checks—brake lights, indicators and so on. Generally, the last person to know the brake lights aren't working is the driver,' he added with a touch of humour, 'so would you please give us a demonstration?'

Rhiannon ground her teeth but complied and the two police officers conducted a leisurely observation of the car in braking and indicating mode.

'Well, that all seems to be working,' Sergeant Daley remarked back at the driver's window. 'Now, if we could just see your licence, please, ma'am?'

Rhiannon closed her eyes then searched through one bag then another before she found her purse. 'Here it is.' She handed it through the window. 'But I haven't changed it over to my married name yet. I—I only got married a few weeks ago.'

'That's fine, ma'am, although you should do so as soon as you can.' He straightened, keeping hold of her licence, and looked over the top of the Mercedes as another car pulled into the lay-by. 'Um—your husband would like to have a word with you, Mrs Richardson, that's all.'

Rhiannon gasped and her eyes flew to the rear-view mirror to see Lee getting out of the four-wheel-drive that had pulled in behind her.

'I don't believe this,' she said. 'I—I…' But she was speechless as Lee came up and opened the door.

'Thanks, Jim and Laura,' Lee said to the two in blue, and handed over his car keys. 'This is really important so I'd appreciate it if you could get my car back to Southall and Rhiannon and I will take the wagon. Would you mind moving over, Rhiannon? I'll drive.'

She opened her mouth to protest but what to say with a police audience already looking wildly speculative?

'How dare you do that?' she did say tautly as Lee drove the Mercedes off smoothly. 'How dare you put the *police* on to me? I told you in my note I'd leave the car at the airport!'

'I didn't put the police *on to* you,' he replied. He'd changed into casual clothes, khaki trousers, a green T-shirt and his leather jacket.

'What would *you* call it then?'

'I know Jim and Laura. They contribute their time extensively to the sports club and I knew they were helping out with traffic control at the church. I simply rang Jim and asked him to be on the lookout for you and to delay you but not to worry you until I got there because something had come up and I needed to find you. I had no concerns about the car at all—it's yours, anyway.'

He changed gear as they came to a section of hairpin bends.

'And you didn't stop to wonder how that was going to look?' she asked bitterly.

He flicked her a fleeting glance. 'Walking out on me was going to "look" bad however you did it, Rhiannon. But apart from Jim and Laura being a bit curious, no other damage has been done. Matt believes you had to go and see your father and he's taken over.'

'Lee, I *am* walking out on you. No, I'm not,' she

cried. 'I'm leaving the way clear for you and Andrea, that's what I'm doing. Don't you see, what we had going for each other would have been OK if everything had been in the past? But it's not and she's free now, and it can only tear *you* apart.'

She took a deep breath and knew she had to find the right key to end this nightmare situation without alerting him to the fact that she was torn apart, otherwise guilt, if nothing else, might see him never let her go and she couldn't bear that.

'Look, what we had was great,' she said huskily, trying desperately to steady herself, 'and I thank you for it, but we can end it quickly and cleanly now and I can go on to other things. After all, it was always more "suitable" than "soul mate" stuff.'

'Was it really?' He looked at her grimly. 'Up at the Bloomfield?'

'Well, I did wonder if there wasn't such a fantasy air to it for a reason. Maybe you needed that kind of approach so you wouldn't think of Andrea—I don't know.' She shrugged. 'But what I'm doing now is what I should have done as soon as I found out who she was.'

'No,' he said harshly, 'it's not, and it's not going to happen now. Tell me one thing: why are you so upset if it's so *suitable* rather than *soul* mate?'

'I—I…' She gestured and took some breaths. 'It's a rather significant change of plan that needs a bit of getting used to, that's all. But, frankly, the quicker it's done the better.'

'Rhiannon—'

'Lee, I saw you look at her, in the passage when you bumped into her back there, back at the wake, and *nothing* will convince me it is over between you two, *nothing*.'

He took a tortured breath but Rhiannon ignored it. 'It—it may take me a few days to organise my father and Di, and it may take a while to pay you back, so if you could bear with me…' She stopped and swallowed as he, almost savagely, drove the car off the road into another lay-by and pulled up with a screech of tyres.

'You're not leaving me for two reasons,' he said, turning to her and looking so dark and intense, she shrank a bit. 'One, there is no place for Andrea in my life, whatever you may like to believe. And secondly, there's no way you can know that you aren't pregnant—or I would know too.'

She paled and her eyes widened. Why hadn't she thought of that?

'Yes, between us, we took a few risks, didn't we?' he queried grimly.

'I…' Rhiannon licked her lips. 'I could check.'

'Why don't you? I'm sure we'll find a chemist open even if it is a Sunday. Mind you,' he warned, 'I still won't let you go whatever the result.'

But Rhiannon was suddenly and frantically counting days in her mind. Was her period overdue? Yes! But only a day or two, maybe three, maybe more! But she had been so busy, could that account for it?

'Rhiannon?' Lee said, more gently, watching her parted lips and stunned eyes. 'Is it possible?'

'Yes,' she whispered. 'Perhaps, but I've been so busy and so *pressured* I didn't even—I—'

'Hush,' he said, taking her hand. 'We will check but don't forget, whatever the result is, we're married and we're going to stay that way.'

She opened her mouth to tell him that if there was no baby he wouldn't be able to stop her from leaving him but in the end held her peace. As it turned out, it would have been a waste of time.

She was pregnant.

Lee had booked them into a luxury Gold Coast resort right on the beach, and he took the news calmly. A lot more calmly than Rhiannon felt.

From the moment the test was positive she fluctuated between heartbreak and hope, from feeling trapped to feeling desperate in case she lost this baby too…

She couldn't even resist when she broke the news and Lee put his arms around her. He might never be hers heart and soul but he would always be the father of her child, she found herself thinking, and at least she wouldn't be alone as she had once before. And, right at that moment, he felt like a tower of strength, something she desperately needed.

'Promise me just one thing, Rhiannon,' he breathed into her hair. 'No more running away from me.'

She rested against him and said tremulously, 'No.'

They stayed on the coast for a week, during which time Rhiannon saw an obstetrician and a gynaecologist.

In light of her previous history, she was warned to take special care of herself, although both doctors could see no reason why she should miscarry again. But she was warned off things like horse-riding and sexual relations, at least until the first trimester was safely behind her.

Lee, who'd insisted on being with her, said nothing to this news. By unspoken agreement, they'd opted for separate beds, anyway. Rhiannon didn't even begin to ask herself why Lee, at least, should have taken that option.

Truth be told, Andrea had faded somewhat from the forefront of her mind, although she did think once that that was the way it had to be in these new circumstances, otherwise she'd drive herself crazy.

And she did say, on the way back from that appointment, 'That's two babies, due within a couple of months of each other.'

'Yes,' he agreed. 'A whole new cycle for the Richardson clan, in duplicate.'

'Lee,' she turned to him impulsively to tell him what Andrea had threatened him with.

But he said quietly, 'Andrea's gone back to France. She has made a life for herself there, she has plenty of friends and she's been left extremely well-off. She's thinking, I believe, of trying her hand at dress design.'

Rhiannon was silent.

He took his hand off the steering wheel and put it over hers. 'Matt was invaluable in all the—negotiations, and he and Mary plan to spend a holiday with her before Mary can't fly. Mary, as you know, gets along with Andrea really well.'

'So the book is closed?' Rhiannon murmured.

'The book is closed. And we can get on with *our* book now.'

But could it ever be closed? she wondered. He had never denied her claim that what she'd seen had shown her things weren't over between him and his beautiful stepmother and they might never be, even if they were to be denied the light of day.

Not that she would have believed him but—it was a road she couldn't afford to travel any longer...

She looked down at his hand covering hers, lean and strong and beautifully shaped, and took a little breath. 'OK.'

CHAPTER NINE

THERE was one girl, so far.

Matt and Mary had a daughter, Tabitha, who had red hair like her mother.

Lee and Rhiannon's baby—they'd decided not to know its sex—was due in a fortnight when Rhiannon ran into the kind of trouble she hadn't foreseen.

It had been, for the most part, a trouble-free pregnancy for Rhiannon. And she had to acknowledge that life had been pleasant in the months since that feverish drive down Mount Tamborine on the day of Ross Richardson's memorial service.

Her father was now fully recovered and he and her aunt had fitted in well not only with the Southall lifestyle but also the arts and crafts community, as well as enjoying the lovely scenery of the hinterland.

In fact, along with Sharon, they'd convened an orchestral society and, with Rhiannon's help and Lee's complete agreement, their outdoor concerts at Southall, the perfect backdrop, were becoming well-known and esteemed.

Rhiannon knew that her father would always have his sad moments but those dangerous tentacles of depression were a thing of the past now.

There had been a tricky moment when he'd discovered Lee's connection to the transport company but by that time he and Lee had become good friends and, with Rhiannon pregnant, he'd been persuaded to let the matter drop.

As for Di, it was becoming more and more apparent that she and Cliff Reinhardt were soul mates, with Christy's approval.

Even Poppy, the pony from hell, had been persuaded to reform her ways to a certain extent, although not thanks to Rhiannon—she was barred from horses. It had been Lee who had turned into a horse whisperer.

Rhiannon had been concerned that he'd be bored spending so much time at Southall, especially when she grew heavy and slow, but she'd underestimated him.

Apparently, for some time he'd been thinking of converting part of Southall's wild acres into an equestrian centre. And that was exactly what he got stuck in and did.

Being barred from horses didn't mean Rhiannon couldn't partake in all the planning stages like stable design, the main barn that would house a showjumping and dressage arena, the horse swimming pool, for example, so it was an interesting time for her too.

And their marriage had settled into a pattern of friendship, even contentment for the most part.

But if Rhiannon had once worried about how to keep the secret core of herself to herself, she no longer had that problem. That special magic that had made it so difficult to conceal her inner self in the first couple of weeks of their marriage was not there now.

Perhaps what became a four-month gap in their sex life and then more caution preached from her doctors, plus the growing evidence of her baby, made it inevitable.

It was probably also inevitable that Andrea Richardson should stalk the byways of her mind, even if only subconsciously.

Whatever, there was, like the flimsiest fabric but there nevertheless, a barrier between them.

To his credit, Lee tried to break through a few times, but when she sensed it she became obscurely agitated and she drew back further.

Then he stopped trying and, quite irrationally, that hurt her, but, as she pointed out to herself, the hormonal highs and lows of pregnancy, the limitations it had put on her because of her past history, demonstrated to her that pregnancy and rationality might not always go hand in hand.

She'd had to spend some time home alone, although that was a relative term once her father and Di moved in, but without Lee, because he refused to allow her to travel with him, particularly outback. But he'd only gone away on the trips he couldn't avoid.

She couldn't deny that, what with her father's and her aunt's endeavours, running Southall and Lee's endeavours, she was leading a busy, useful even colourful life, if not quite as active as she was used to.

She couldn't deny that her marriage had fallen almost exactly into the parameters she herself had set. They liked and trusted each other in every area but one, they were building a good life on common ground, they'd soon be a family.

It was only very occasionally that the odd thought pricked the fabric of that barrier she'd erected like a thorn going into her heart.

Such as, the only difference from those parameters

she'd laid down was her vow that she'd never marry anyone who could hurt her the way she'd been hurt before; her stance that she wouldn't expect to be fallen madly in love with, nor would she be doing that.

Famous last words, she couldn't help herself from reflecting occasionally. Had she really believed them? Or had she been fooling herself even way back then?

But for the most part, she was able to bury those painful thoughts.

And it was only when Lee was away that she sometimes couldn't help herself from wanting more...

Then, with two weeks to go, Mary unwittingly opened a can of worms for Rhiannon.

She, Matt and Tabitha were spending the weekend at Southall. Winter was drawing in and they were sitting in the den in front of a roaring log fire.

Tabitha, now three months old, had been put to bed—contrary to some expectations, Mary Richardson had taken to motherhood like a duck to water and she was full of advice.

But advice was not the nature of the bombshell she dropped that wet, windy evening.

'Listen up, guys,' she said, 'I've had a fantastic idea. When your baby arrives, Rhiannon, let's have a double christening of the century here at Southall. I've already sounded it out with Andrea and she agrees it's a great idea—she was going to come home for a visit anyway so it might as well be for the christening!'

Rhiannon stared at her with parted lips and stunned eyes.

Matt opened his mouth to speak but closed it.

Lee said, 'No, Mary. Rhiannon and I have other plans.'

'What plans? Why?' Mary tossed her red curls. 'Oh, come on, Lee, don't tell me you still haven't forgiven Andrea for marrying your father?'

'Not at all—and we'll let you know when we've made them. Is—' he paused and listened '—is that your baby I hear, Mary?'

'Yes, it is. Come on, darling, we might have an early night.' Matt reached for Mary's hand and took her away.

Lee got up and closed the door behind them. 'Some things never change about Mary,' he said as he sat down opposite Rhiannon and put another log on the fire.

'She doesn't know—*does* she know now about you and Andrea?' Rhiannon rephrased.

'No, only you—unless Matt's worked it out.'

'Wouldn't he tell her?'

'I doubt it. He may be besotted but I'm pretty sure he wouldn't do that to me.'

Rhiannon suffered an extraordinary "contrary" sensation, as in *'Mary, Mary, quite contrary'*—by a different name.

She tried to analyse where it had come from. She was sleeping badly at the moment; it was difficult to get comfortable. She sometimes felt as if she'd been pregnant for years and it would never end. She often felt ungainly and she couldn't believe that anyone, but particularly Lee, could see her as anything but bloated as well as ungainly.

Or was it the mention of Andrea that had done it, and that smooth, brick-wall façade of Lee's in response?

Whatever it was, she discovered she was thoroughly annoyed with Lee, only it was worse than that.

Every little grievance she'd ever cherished against him welled up inside her. His—always—superior attitude towards his sister-in-law…yes, Mary might have had some flighty ways but she was turning into both a good wife and mother.

His—she sought for the right word—his *dominance* over all and sundry. Not only what his brother would not do to him but also all the brick walls she'd run into with him. Every last one of them right down, she thought tempestuously, to being able to make use of the local police to stop her running away from him, not to mention the fact that he'd only had to postulate the possibility that she was pregnant, and—heigh-ho!—she was.

No, she cautioned herself, that's being ridiculous, we did take chances—but in the next second she thought, I don't care! I've had enough and all I want to do is exactly the opposite of what he wants!

Even the sight of him, so tall and beautifully made in his navy jumper with patches and fawn cords, was suddenly anathema to her.

'Lee,' she said, masking the anger in her eyes with difficulty, 'I think it would be a good idea, a double christening. I'd love to organise it and we do have to break the ice with Andrea some time.'

He paused and watched her narrowly. 'Are you trying to tell me something, Rhiannon?'

'Yes!' she said with completely false, calm surety, 'I want to do this and I'm going to. So you might like to tell Mary you've changed your mind.'

As she finished speaking, she dispensed with calm surety and she didn't bother to mask the blaze of hostility in her eyes as she looked across at Lee.

'Rhiannon,' he said evenly, 'listen to me, I need to—'

But she broke in furiously, 'Oh, no, you don't! Just go away, Lee. I'll be much better on my own at the moment.'

He studied her for a long time then got up and walked out.

She slept, locked in, in a guest bedroom that night, although "slept" was only a notional term. She was racked alternately by confusion and anger. It was as if someone had lit a slow fuse within her. On the other hand, why on earth would she want a double christening with Andrea present?

She must have been mad but it had seemed so important at the time to defy Lee *somehow*.

Another thought that touched her was—had the seeds of this rebellion been simmering in her for a long time? Was it even a rebellion against the fact that she'd done exactly what she'd sworn never to do— fallen in love with a man who could hurt her?

She looked pale and unwell the next morning and, after Matt and Mary had left, Lee cornered her in his mother's study.

'Rhiannon, we have to have this out. It's not good for you or the baby to be—'

'I'm fine,' she denied.

His gaze wandered over her face and her full figure under stretch tights and a long jumper. 'You don't look it.'

'Well, physically I am fine, and for the most part I enjoy my role—'

'What role?'

She shrugged. 'The happy housekeeper who ended up in the boss's bed. I know, I know,' she added as he moved convulsively, 'I made my bed—let's not miss the opportunity to use a good old cliché!'

'Have I ever made you feel like that?' he queried harshly.

'No,' she conceded. 'The opposite sometimes, as if I'm a fantasy creature who—'

'Rhiannon,' he interrupted in a hard voice.

'But I'm getting sick and tired of you calling all the shots, Lee.'

'Because I didn't agree to a three-ring-circus kind of christening?' he shot at her. 'Or could it be that your aversion to hearing anything other than *your* version of the truth has rebounded on you?'

She gasped. 'I have not!'

'Then listen to me now. Andrea—'

But Rhiannon put her hands over her ears and walked out.

It rained all day and looked set to keep on all night, torrential rain and high winds that tore down trees and turned some roads into raging torrents.

There was no one else on the estate but Lee and Rhiannon. Her father and Di had gone to Brisbane with the orchestral society; Cliff and Christy were on holiday, Sharon had been told not to brave the tempest.

It was an uncomfortable day otherwise.

Somewhat ashamed of her childish behaviour but still possessed of that slow-burning fuse, Rhiannon kept out of Lee's way. That wasn't hard to do, he was out checking the estate and the new work of the equestrian centre most of the morning, then he got involved in the rescue of a car and its occupants from a nearby swollen creek that had flooded a bridge.

She put his dinner in the oven and waited up for him for a while.

He'd told her, before going out, to call him on his mobile if she needed him.

'I'll be fine. I've got another two weeks to go and Mary,' she broke off and bit her lip then soldiered on, 'is of the opinion I haven't "dropped" sufficiently yet.'

Something flickered in his eyes. 'Just stay put and ring me if anything happens.'

Nothing happened as the solid old house resisted the worst of the weather, making her feel warm and safe. And really sorry for those caught in the might of the storm and those who were rescuing them.

And she did try to wait up for Lee, only to fall asleep on the settee in the den in front of the fire before he came home.

She couldn't identify what woke her but it was to see Lee sitting opposite her, watching her.

He'd obviously showered and changed into clean clothes.

'Oh,' she sat up with her hand to her back, 'did you rescue them? What's it like out there?'

'Yes, they're safe and sound. But it's wet and you can't get in or out of Southall at the moment other than on foot or horseback. There are trees down everywhere and two creeks cutting the road.' He stopped then swore quietly as the lights flickered and went out. 'I was afraid that was on the cards so I've got some gas lamps and kerosene ones ready. The phone lines are also down.'

Rhiannon grimaced then put her hand to her back again and thought—Braxton-Hicks? No, this feels different—oh, surely not!

But surely yes—her waters broke right on cue.

'Rhiannon?' Lee got up and came to squat in front
of her. 'What is it?' he asked urgently.

'The baby's coming,' she breathed. 'Oh, Lee, what
a night for it. We won't be able to go anywhere or—'

'We'll be fine.' He took her hand and looked into
her eyes steadily. 'We can still get out by phone on the
mobile so we can get in touch with emergency
services. I'm going to do that right now; you just relax
and time the contractions. We've probably got hours
yet. Here.' He took off his watch and handed it to her
then he touched her cheek. 'Hang in there, secretary-
general.'

The strangest thought flew through Rhiannon's
mind. It was the first time he'd referred to their honeymoon since she'd tried to run away. Did it mean…?
What did it mean?

Half an hour later, they'd learnt that a helicopter
evacuation might be possible but not for a couple of
hours; the weather was too wild to attempt it at the
moment. But Lee had been patched through to a
doctor, who gave it as his opinion that they did have
quite a few hours up their sleeve, especially with a first
baby, but they should be prepared for anything all the
same.

So Lee made some preparations. Because the den
was warmest and had added light from its log fire, he
brought in a bed and transferred Rhiannon to it. He
helped her change into a loose, comfortable nightgown. Then he put on hand some clean towels, soap
and a bowl of water and he boiled a pair of scissors on
a portable gas stove he dug out, causing Rhiannon to
thank her lucky stars that Southall did have everything
that opened and shut.

He also brewed them a cup of tea.

He said with a faint smile, when all this was accomplished and the contractions were about ten minutes apart and quite bearable, 'Thanks to all those excruciatingly embarrassing pre-natal classes you dragged me along to, I know what I'm doing to a certain extent.'

'I didn't drag you,' she protested then smiled ruefully. 'But yes, they were a bit hard to take in public.'

'I've also done this before, if it comes to that.'

'Done…?' She raised her head and blinked at him.

He laughed at her expression. 'I've delivered a foal and two calves in my time, there have to be some similarities.' He paused and grimaced. 'You may not feel it was appropriate to mention that but—you can trust me not to fold under pressure.'

'I do,' she whispered.

They listened to the rain and the wind in silence for a while.

Then, looking into the fire, Lee said, 'The only person who ever brought a distant shore and a bonfire to mind was you, Rhiannon. You did make me feel as if I was capturing you, you did—you had an elusive siren quality that frustrated me and teased at me and made me want you in spite of everything else.

'It was just you, nothing else,' he went on, 'well, us, and I can't tell you how much I've missed it. It was like a magic thread between us.'

She stared at him and saw the pain in his eyes, the lines of strain beside his mouth, and she opened her mouth but tensed.

'A bit stronger, that one?' he hazarded.

She let out a slow, shuddering breath as the pain subsided.

He waited for a couple of minutes, holding her hand, then he said, 'Can I tell you something? There's nowhere else I would rather be than helping you through this, nowhere. There's *no* one I'd rather be with. Yes, I did bump into Andrea after my father's memorial service, and yes, for a moment, everything she'd once done to me came back. But you have no idea how fast that all changed.'

'Lee?' She stared at him again, frowning.

'It started when I went looking for you and found your pearls on your pillow, and your note. One minute I was looking into the past, the next minute, virtually, I was seeing an empty, desolate shore. I couldn't believe what a catalyst that turned out to be. The thought of losing you suddenly hit me for six. Hold hard, my darling, beloved, Rhiannon,' he added as she tensed again. 'Try to breathe as they showed you—there, it's going.' But he looked at his watch on the pillow with a little frown.

'That was a bit closer together,' she breathed.

'Yes, but still eight minutes. Are you comfortable now?'

She nodded then sat up incredulously. 'Tell me—tell me about this catalyst.'

'It was as if the Andrea I once thought I'd loved went away, as if she wasn't real, and never had been. All that remained were her…machinations and the fact that she may have lost me you—my true reality, so warm-hearted, so generous, so genuine, so sane but also so desirable.' He paused and shook his head. 'I suddenly knew she had no power over me any more, it was over, and over because of you.'

'You didn't tell me this when—when you caught up with me, Lee,' Rhiannon said with an effort.

'No. I was going to,' he said quietly, 'but would you have believed me?'

Rhiannon looked back down the nearly nine months that had intervened, to her iron-clad certainty that Lee still loved Andrea, and she said on a long, slow breath, 'No.'

'I couldn't blame you. I wasn't even sure I could explain it properly, but what really slew me and took the wind right out of my sails,' he looked down at her hand in his, 'was that you seemed so sure, on your side anyway, that what was between us was suitable rather than soul-mate stuff, a bargain, that's all. And you usually mean what you say. So I decided to take another tack. I thought, OK, I'll show her that we are soul mates. But you resisted me every step of the way.

'And,' he went on, 'I got my own medical advice. In light of what had happened before and all the emotional turmoil you'd suffered at the time, it seemed certain that you'd be very vulnerable to any stress. So I decided to bide my time, I decided that the most important thing was to get you safely through this pregnancy in the way *you* seemed to be able to handle best.'

Rhiannon swallowed. 'Oh, Lee—' She broke off and started to sweat.

'Here we go again,' he murmured and wiped her face with a hand towel. 'Breathe—breathe in time with me, sweetheart, we can do this together.'

And somehow, as he concentrated on breathing with her, somehow they became one and she knew he was passing confidence and strength through to her and she clung to it and used it to fend off the worst of the pain.

This time, when the contraction passed, Rhiannon

discovered there were tears on her cheeks, but not tears of pain and sadness as she thought that perhaps no other scenario would have made her believe what Lee was telling her but this one.

Because no man who didn't love her could infuse his strength, his compassion for her into her heart the way he did.

'I did—it did seem the only way I could handle it but that was…' She stopped and gripped his hand. 'I may not have wanted to let you see it but I've—loved you for a long time, almost from the beginning. That's why I wanted to run away, because I was hurting so badly. This—this is nothing in comparison.'

There, I've said it at last, she thought.

'Do you mean that, Rhiannon?'

'Oh, yes, yes!' she whispered intensely.

'What a bloody fool I've been,' he marvelled and she saw the lines of strain leave his face, saw the relaxation of his muscles. 'But you did seem to be holding me at arm's length.'

'Only as self-protection. If you must know,' she smiled shakily, 'I've wept oceans of tears over you in secret.'

He closed his eyes then cupped her face and kissed her gently. But suddenly a new concern came to his eyes. 'Only yesterday—only this morning you looked as if you hated me.'

'I did a little,' she confessed. 'But I was tired of being pregnant, I was tired of thinking I was the one in love, not you, I was—I thought you were so definite about the christening because of Andrea.'

'No. I'm simply not a fan of those kind of overrated dos.' He grimaced. 'Sorry, Mary.' He lifted Rhiannon's hand and kissed her knuckles. 'I love you, I—*love* you.'

'I love you too,' she whispered, and went into his arms, where she could hear his heart beating heavily, as if his anguish still hadn't quite left him. 'Believe me, Lee,' she said. 'I know I was—I've been difficult—'

'Pregnant, actually,' he said into her hair.

'Maybe.' She sniffed. 'But the stupid part of it was, whilst I guessed you stopped trying to get through to me because it upset me, and it did, it also hurt when you stopped. I've been a mass of contradictions!'

'So what makes you believe me now?' he queried.

'The way you're doing this. It makes me feel as if I'm your north and south, as if you're my tower of strength, as if we're one.'

'Thank God,' he said with a heartfelt sigh, and he held her as if he'd never let her go.

But unborn babies on the move make no concessions even for such heart-stopping events as these, and when they drew apart it was to deal with another contraction.

'Is it my imagination or are things really speeding up?' she asked raggedly.

'Yes, they are.' He got up. 'I'm going to have a look and talk to the doctor. Try to relax.'

'For the moment, I feel as if I'm on cloud nine.'

'That may change but we'll get back there, never fear.'

It did change as the contractions speeded up and intensified, and she heard through her fog of pain this time Lee telling the doctor that she appeared to be fully dilated, and he left the line open.

'OK, we could be on the last lap.' He came back to her side. 'The doctor reckons you've just about broken all the records for a first birth! But now you need to do what I tell you—it's going to either be pant or push. OK? Think you can cope?'

'Yes,' she gasped, and they held hands tightly for a moment.

Three contractions later, the baby girl who was to be named Reese Margaret Richardson after her grandmothers made her entry into the world.

'Another girl!' Lee told her. 'Blonde, too, I'd say, like her mum, and a real little tiger about getting born anyway.'

'Is she—is she all right?' Rhiannon asked, echoing every mother's first query.

'Looks fine to me—Rhiannon, I'm going to give you the phone, darling, so you can relay the doctor's instructions on to me. Oh,' he said, as an infant wail rose, 'she's done that bit herself—an intelligent baby obviously, but why wouldn't she be with the parents she has?'

Rhiannon smiled joyfully then lifted the phone to her ear and spoke to the doctor on the other end.

'Well done, Rhiannon!' he congratulated her. 'Now, here's what Lee needs to do.'

Not many minutes later, Lee presented her with baby Reese wrapped in a towel. He washed his hands again and he collapsed into the chair beside the bed. 'I need a drink. I don't think I've ever needed a drink as much as I do now. Hang on,' he ran a hand through his hair and a smile grew in his eyes. 'Well, look at you two,' he said softly, as Rhiannon cuddled her baby with her heart in her eyes.

She put out her hand and he put his into it.

'We three,' she said. 'Thank you so much. For loving me, for everything you did, but for loving me back.'

'Always, Rhiannon.' He closed his eyes.

* * *

'Lee!' Rhiannon said a year later to the day. 'It's not *my* birthday.'

'No,' he agreed, 'but it was quite a day last year. Not only, between us, did we deliver our baby but it was also the first day of the rest of our lives, wouldn't you agree?'

They were in bed, having not long ago woken to Reese's first birthday.

They were naked but deliciously warm beneath a goose-feather duvet—it was a wet, cold day again— and he'd just handed her another black leather box tooled with gold.

Rhiannon clicked the catch and drew a breath as a pair of earrings was revealed. South Sea pearls again, beautifully set in a gold and pave-set diamond rim to match the clasp on her strand of pearls—which she just happened to be wearing.

'Oh, they're beautiful and they match so well, the pearls! How did you manage that?'

'I bought them at the same time and kept them in reserve for just such an occasion. You know,' he lay back and rubbed his forehead with the back of his hand, 'since that's how we first made love, I became really addicted to you in earrings and a necklace—and nothing else.'

'Ah.' She tucked her hair behind her ears and put the earrings on. 'There. I suppose I could say I'm—well-dressed for the occasion now.'

'Mmm…' He traced the line of her necklace down to her breasts with his fingers and let them stray.

'If there's one thing I'm addicted to about you,' she said and stopped to study him, his dishevelled dark hair, the stubble on his jaw, the heavy-lidded way he was looking at her, the strength of his shoulders and chest.

'Go on. Only one?'

'Well,' her lips curved, 'one of them. You're divine with designer stubble.'

He rubbed his jaw ruefully. 'There's nothing designer about it, it just happens.'

'Maybe, but it does strange things to me.' She leant lightly on his chest. 'So,' she looked into the deep blue of his eyes, 'here I am, feeling all siren again. I think it must have something to do with all these South Sea pearls,' she told him gravely. 'Want me to do anything about it? It would be a lovely way to say thank you. Last night, after all, *was* about eight hours ago.'

He took a tortured breath and growled something indecipherable in his throat. But as his hands curved on her breasts, a piping little voice made itself heard from the room next door.

Both Lee and Rhiannon closed their eyes in comic frustration.

'There's always tonight,' he said after giving her a quick, hard kiss. 'Put your nightgown on…I'll get her. Just one thing.' He got out of bed and pulled on pyjama bottoms. 'Has the Siren's Union really given this marriage its seal of approval, Rhiannon?'

She paused with her nightgown in her hands. 'It's given it ten out of ten, five stars, *cum laude*—didn't you know?' she asked, her eyes alight with love and laughter.

He gave her another kiss. 'Just like to check now and then.'

Rhiannon pulled her nightgown on and lay back, more contented, more in love than she'd ever thought possible.

Then she started to smile as she heard the conversation coming from the nursery, and really felt as if her cup was running over.

'Hi, tiger! Sleep well?' Lee's deep voice filled with teasing affection.

'Daddy, Daddy, Daddy!' Reese's little voice, filled with pure joy.

Harlequin®

Mediterranean NIGHTS™

Tycoon Elias Stamos is launching his newest luxury cruise ship from his home port in Greece. But someone from his past is eager to expose old secrets and to see the Stamos empire crumble.

Mediterranean Nights launches in June 2007 with...

FROM RUSSIA, WITH LOVE
by *Ingrid Weaver*

Join the guests and crew of *Alexandra's Dream* as they are drawn into a world of glamour, romance and intrigue in this new 12-book series.

www.eHarlequin.com

MN1

REQUEST YOUR FREE BOOKS!

2 FREE NOVELS
PLUS 2
FREE GIFTS!

YES! Please send me 2 FREE Harlequin Presents® novels and my 2 FREE gifts. After receiving them, if I don't wish to receive any more books, I can return the shipping statement marked "cancel." If I don't cancel, I will receive 6 brand-new novels every month and be billed just $3.80 per book in the U.S., or $4.47 per book in Canada, plus 25¢ shipping and handling per book and applicable taxes, if any*. That's a savings of close to 15% off the cover price! I understand that accepting the 2 free books and gifts places me under no obligation to buy anything. I can always return a shipment and cancel at any time. Even if I never buy another book from Harlequin, the two free books and gifts are mine to keep forever.

106 HDN EEXK   306 HDN EEXV

Name	(PLEASE PRINT)	
Address		Apt. #
City	State/Prov.	Zip/Postal Code

Signature (if under 18, a parent or guardian must sign)

Mail to the **Harlequin Reader Service®**:
IN U.S.A.: P.O. Box 1867, Buffalo, NY 14240-1867
IN CANADA: P.O. Box 609, Fort Erie, Ontario L2A 5X3

Not valid to current Harlequin Presents subscribers.

Want to try two free books from another line?
Call 1-800-873-8635 or visit www.morefreebooks.com.

* Terms and prices subject to change without notice. NY residents add applicable sales tax. Canadian residents will be charged applicable provincial taxes and GST. This offer is limited to one order per household. All orders subject to approval. Credit or debit balances in a customer's account(s) may be offset by any other outstanding balance owed by or to the customer. Please allow 4 to 6 weeks for delivery.

Your Privacy: Harlequin is committed to protecting your privacy. Our Privacy Policy is available online at www.eHarlequin.com or upon request from the Reader Service. From time to time we make our lists of customers available to reputable firms who may have a product or service of interest to you. If you would prefer we not share your name and address, please check here. ☐

HP07

Mediterranean Brides

**Two billionaires, one Greek, one Spanish—
will they claim their unwilling brides?**

Meet Sandor and Miguel, men who've taken all the prizes
when it comes to looks, power, wealth and arrogance.
Now they want marriage with two beautiful women.
But this time, for the first time, both Mediterranean
billionaires have met their matches and it will take more
than money or cool to tame their unwilling mistresses—
try seduction, passion and possession!

Eleanor Wentworth has always been unloved and
unwanted. Greek tycoon Sandor Christofides has wealth
and acclaim—all he needs is Eleanor as his bride.
But is Ellie just a pawn in the billionaire's game?

BOUGHT:
THE GREEK'S BRIDE
by Lucy Monroe

On sale June 2007.